HIGHWAY THROUGH HELL

The T-Force Thriller Series Book Three

Charles Whiting

SAPERE
BOOKS

HIGHWAY THROUGH HELL

Published by Sapere Books.

24 Trafalgar Road, Ilkley, LS29 8HH

saperebooks.com

ISBN: 978-0-85495-411-7

'So they've got us surrounded, the poor bastards!'
Anonymous GI in Bastogne, December 22nd, 1944.

PART ONE: ATTACK!

'Up there in Belgium, we're fighting in the dark. All I know is that one whole Kraut army is heading like a bat outa hell for Bastogne. Hardt, you've got to plough through that Army and find a route for my Fourth Armoured… It's Bastogne or bust by Christmas.'

General Patton to Major Hardt, CO, T-Force December 17th, 1944.

CHAPTER 1

It was bitterly cold. An icy December wind swept across the white Northern French border countryside. Time and time again, the GIs, crouched in the slowly advancing armoured vehicles, blinked their eyes to force away the tears. Now the sickly yellow winter sun had slid across the bleak horizon and hung poised there, as if undecided whether it should rise any further. Long, black, sinister shadows raced across the gleaming surface of the deep snow.

In the back of the little Wasp, positioned in the middle of the armoured sweep, Limey, T-Force's radio operator, turned his crimson, frozen face to the sun's weak yellow rays, desperate to catch even the slightest warmth. 'Cor ferk a duck, Major!' he groaned, his breath fogging the icy air, 'it looks like a ruddy Woolworth's penny Christmas card. But it's sodding cold enough to freeze the balls off a brass monkey! That's for sure.' He shivered dramatically and blew hard on his frozen finger tips.

Major Hardt, T-Force's lean, hard-faced commander, standing upright at the front of the Wasp, next to its terrible weapon, nodded, but said nothing. His whole attention was concentrated on the enemy held countryside ahead. It did look empty and as peaceful as a cheap pre-war Christmas card, with two-foot icicles gleaming from the shell-shattered telegraph poles and with deep snow capping the firs, running along the ridges on both sides of the armoured reconnaissance force. But he knew the calm was deceptive. Running along the length of the horizon was the strongest network of fortifications, ever constructed by man — the Kraut Siegfried Line — soon to be attacked by General Patton's Third Army.

For four years since the German victory in 1940, it had been empty. But now that the Third was poised on the frontier of the Reich, ready to smash Hitler's Germany apart, the enemy had hurriedly manned it again. The problem was that Third Army Intelligence knew absolutely nothing of the strength of those forces; and for weeks now the Third had not taken a deserter prisoner, the usual source of Intelligence information. Indeed as Colonel Koch, Patton's Chief of Intelligence, had told Hardt when he had briefed the Major for this mission: the whole 100 mile long American Army front had yielded exactly *five* prisoners since the First of December 1944. 'We can't goddam fight in the dark, Hardt! That's why I want T-Force to get on up to the Saar front. I want prisoners.' The bespectacled Intelligence man had slapped the desk in front of him impatiently. '*Major, I want heads and mouths!*'

Hardt raised his binoculars and focused them once again on the white waste ahead. The first Kraut bunkers would be in the woods ahead. For all he knew the enemy was following the progress of the T-Force vehicles crawling through the snow already, ready to open up once they got in range. But it was not Hardt's intention to sacrifice his men testing their strength in order to get a few prisoners. He wanted a softer target. Carefully he swept his front. Then he spotted it — a row of haystacks, their tops heavy with snow. Why he asked himself, as he tried to detect any movement in or around them, would any farmer in his right mind leave them out to be ruined by the winter weather? The answer was obvious. The haystacks concealed the first Kraut outposts. Swiftly he made up his mind. He would attack the seemingly innocent piles of hay.

With luck they would yield the precious 'heads and mouths' that Colonel Koch wanted.

'Limey,' he rapped.

'Sir,' the little Cockney answered smartly.

'Get on to Red and Lieutenant van Fleet. Tell 'em I'm going to hit those haystacks at eleven o'clock. When I flame them and the Krauts start to bug out, I want them to come in from both flanks and grab as many as they can. *But quick!*

'Wilco, sir,' Limey sang out, his coldness forgotten now, as he contacted the half-tracks, filled with the rest of T-Force to their left and right flanks. Five minutes later they started to rumble forward across the glittering snow, with Major Hardt, suddenly feeling absurdly like Don Quixote about to tilt at windmills…

The little tracked Wasp came to a halt seventy-five yards away from the first haystack. There was no sound save the rumble of the heavy artillery in the far distance, the ever present background music of war, and the soft clatter of the half-tracks on the snow to their flanks. Behind Hardt, Limey was singing monotonously, 'You'll be far better off in a home, far better off in a home,' over and over again.

Hardt bit his lip. Why didn't the Krauts open fire? The Wasp was a sitting duck, completely out in the open, silhouetted stark black against the glittering white of the snow. Was he going to make a fool of himself? Would he use the new and terrible British weapon, which Limey had acquired for T-Force in his usual mysterious and undoubtedly dishonest way, for nothing? Were the haystacks simply haystacks, left out to rot by some farmer who had fled his farm before the advancing Americans!

'Well, there's only one way to find out, sir.' It was Limey, grinning up at him cheekily. 'What is it you Yanks say — pee or get off the pot!'

'You're too goddam clever by half, Limey!' Hardt snapped. But he knew the little Englishman was right. 'All right, gunner,' he commanded the gunner, squeezed in between him and the driver, 'prepare to fire.'

The GI needed no urging. He swung up the terrible weapon. 'Ready, sir!'

Hardt took a deep breath. 'Okay — flame 'em!'

The gunner pressed the trigger. There was a great hush like some primeval monster drawing a huge breath. A long tongue of scarlet flame licked out alarmingly, its edges tinged with black oily smoke. It curled round the first haystack. Its heavy cap of snow disappeared in an instant. A moment later it was burning fiercely, the smoke streaming up into the hard blue winter sky. But no terrified, screaming victim emerged from the sudden holocaust!

'Hit the next bastard, gunner!' Hardt cried above the crackle of the flames. 'And make it snappy!'

The gunner swung round his gun. He pressed the trigger. Again that terrible stream of all-consuming flame shot out. It wreathed itself around the pile of straw. In a flash the haystack was burning fiercely, and something which had once been a man was staggering across the snow, writhing and jerking convulsively, trying to escape the stifling, searing horror.

'They're in there, sir!' Limey cried excitedly, as another field-grey uniformed, burning figure tumbled out of the haystack, his tunic on fire. Blinded by the ever-mounting flames, the soldier staggered forward a few paces, his outstretched arm burning furiously, to sprawl full-length in the furiously hissing snow, shrivelling up before the horrified Americans' eyes.

'Cease firing, gunner!' Hardt croaked as more and more Germans scrambled furiously from the remaining haystacks and flinging away their weapons in absolute panic, began to stumble through the deep snow to the rear. 'Let Red and Lieutenant van Fleet take care of them.' He nodded to the flanks where the half-tracks were already rattling in to cut off the fleeing Germans. Suddenly he turned and began to vomit over the side of the little Wasp.

Fighting for control, Major Hardt, followed by Limey, crunched through the snow to examine the bodies, still smouldering in the glowing hay. An arm loomed up, looking like the charred and shrivelled crook of a tree root. At first at least. But when Hardt got closer to it, he could make out the hump of a body attached to it, shrunk to the size of a pygmy by the intense heat.

'Not much left of that bugger,' Limey said. 'You certainly toasted his nuts for him, Major!'

Hardt could not speak; he was too horrified by the results of his own work. The bodies lay in naked, blackened heaps, frozen by the terrible flame into grotesque poses, only their boots and their coalscuttle helmets remaining. He forced himself to bend down close to one of the Germans who had been splashed with the liquid as he had attempted to make his escape from the second burning haystack. The German's helmet had fallen off and now he lay there, his lower body intact, but with his black eyeballs, naked, charred and somehow obscene, staring up at the man who had killed him almost contemptuously.

'Pretty old boy,' Limey expressed his own thought, 'and look at his boots! Not even a pair of jackboots, just old walking-out shoes, soled with tyre rubber. Old Jerry must be badly off for blokes to be putting that kind in the line, especially when they know Old Blood an' Guts Patton is in the area.'

Hardt conquered his revulsion. 'Yes, you're right there, Limey. We all know Hitler's scraping the barrel. But surely he wouldn't attempt to defend the Siegfried Line with that kind of guy!' Puzzled he stared down at the still smoking body. 'Hell, General Patton could walk through that kind of opposition — with one arm tied behind his back!'

'You can sure say that again, sir,' Big Red's deep voice broke in. 'Look at these beauts we just rounded up.'

Hardt spun round. Together with the big lumbering Dutchie Schulze, T-Force's interpreter, Master Sergeant 'Big Red' Carstens, armed with a grease gun, was urging forward their prisoners: two astonishingly old men in sloppy field-grey, who looked like Turks, and a bespectacled, narrow-chested youth, one lens of his glasses cracked into a gleaming spider's web.

'Christ,' Limey breathed in awe, 'bloody Laurel and Hardy and their Dad!'

'Yeah,' Big Red said contemptuously, 'that's what we thought. Christ on a crutch, these guys aren't fit for service* — and then some!' He spat drily onto the scuffed surface of the snow. 'Brother, old man Hitler is sure hard up!'

'They don't even speak Kraut,' Dutchie added in his usual ponderous manner. 'The fat guys at least... It's some lingo that I don't understand.'

'What about the kid?' Hardt asked, nodding at the bespectacled youth, who had now recovered his breath and was staring at his captors fiercely through one half of his glasses.

'*Was ist Ihre Einheit?*' — Dutchie began, but the boy cut him short with an angry wave of his dirty hand.

'Speak not German with me,' he said in understandable, if ungrammatical English. 'I speak English. What is it you are wishing to know?'

Weakling though the boy might be, Hardt thought, sizing him up for a moment, he certainly wasn't afraid of his captors like the other two PWs. They were trembling all over, as if Big Red might mow them down with his grease gun at any moment. Indeed there was something almost offensively aggressive on the boy's pale grey face. 'What is the nationality of these men?' he indicated the two fat men and asked his question slowly so that boy could not fail to understand. The German shrugged, carelessly. 'Who knows — and who cares? They make good cannon fodder. They serve their purpose.'

Hardt looked at the boy sharply. 'What do you mean — *serve their purpose?*'

The boy grinned knowingly. 'That you would like to know, Mister American, eh?' He wagged a dirty, skinny finger at Hardt in the German fashion. 'But from me, you get nothing.'

'Shall I work the little, four-eyed crud over, sir?' Big Red grunted and doubled his fist, his face a beetroot red with sudden anger. 'I could take the bastard apart as if he's made of crackers.'

'No, let Intelligence — Major Hardt began. But he never finished the sentence. Suddenly on the horizon a red signal flare hushed into the hard blue sky. It was followed an instant later by a frightening, earth-shaking roar. With a hoarse, exultant scream, a salvo of enemy shells tore the morning stillness apart.

'Incoming mail!' Dutchie Schulze cried and flung himself full length in the snow, followed with surprising speed by the two Turkish-looking prisoners, as the first shells ripped up huge holes, like the work of some gigantic mole, to their front. An instant later, the rest joined them on the snow, as the earth quaked and quivered beneath them like a live thing. All except the bespectacled German. It was the chance he had been waiting for. Suddenly he pelted forward. The T-Force driver, cowering at the side of the Wasp, hands over his ears to protect them from the blast, saw him when it was too late. He tried to draw his forty-five. The German was quicker. His boot lashed out and caught the driver squarely in the face. He reeled back screaming, nose broken, great gobs of gleaming blood splattering the white surface of the snow.

In a flash the German was behind the wheel of the little armoured vehicle. He crashed home first gear. Its tracks slipped frantically in the loose snow. Big Red sprang to his feet.

'*Stop where you are!*' he bellowed.

The boy was not listening. The Wasp started to rumble forward. Big Red aimed from the hip.

'Don't shoot, Red!' Hardt screamed. 'We want the bastard alive and kicking!'

Too late! The stream of armour-piercing bullets riddled the thin sides of the Wasp. A slug hit the fuel tank. A great whoosh. The vehicle hurtled high in the air with the force of the explosion, as if thrown by some gigantic hand. The shattered wreck came down a moment later, burning furiously, the German boy sprawled dead over the broken steering wheel, the flames already licking greedily at his clothing. As the German shelling ceased, leaving behind it a loud, echoing silence, Limey rose slowly to his feet, dusted the snow from his clothing and said: 'Well, Major, there goes the Wasp — and little laughing boy as well. It looks as if Intelligence will have to start reading bleeding tea leaves if they want to know what's going on behind the Jerry lines this sodding Christmas.'

Tunelessly whistling the hit of the year, *I'm Dreaming of a White Christmas*, he began to plod through the deep snow to the unconscious Wasp driver, leaving a saddened Major Hardt nodding his bald head in helpless agreement.

CHAPTER 2

'Tough luck, Hardt,' Colonel Koch said wearily. 'We sure could have used that Kraut.' Outside Patton's HQ it was snowing softly, muffling the tread of the sentries, and the sad, wintry mood seemed to have infected the tubby, bespectacled 3rd Army Chief of Intelligence. 'Info from the Kraut side of the line seems to have about dried up completely. As the doughs say — it's situation snafu.'

Hardt smiled faintly, hearing the GI expression coming from Koch. 'I'm sorry, sir. The little Kraut was quicker than we were,' he said. 'But what about the two Turkish-looking guys?'

Koch shook his head. 'No dice. They're Turcomen, ex-Red Army guys, captured by the Krauts and recruited into their army. They don't speak German and they don't speak Russian, only their own Godforsaken lingo. All the interrogators in the HQ Cage can get out of them is a look of absolute fear and what seems to be the words in German — *big boom-boom come soon.*'

Hardt flashed Koch and the keen-looking Major standing attentively behind him a swift look. 'Trouble, Colonel?'

'Sure,' Koch answered wearily. 'Trouble and plenty of it, you betcha!'

'But Colonel,' Hardt protested. 'Everybody knows the Krauts are beaten — kaput. Just look at the quality of those guys we pulled in — an 'unfit to serve' and two fat guys who are old enough to be my father — and they were defending Germany's last major defensive line! Surely, if that's the kind of human material they've got left, they've had it?'

'So you think so, Major?' Koch took off his gold-rimmed eyeglasses and wiped his eyes wearily. Outside some top sergeant was snarling, 'I'm not gonna tell you Joes again! Get the lead outa ya asses, willya?' The Intelligence Chief replaced his glasses and looked at Hardt with a new light in his faded eyes. 'As you know Hardt, I try to present the Commanding General with a daily appreciation of enemy units up to one hundred and fifty miles to both the right and left flanks of Third Army?'

Hardt nodded. His own élite special reconnaissance outfit, T-Force, played a major part in obtaining that intelligence for Koch.

'Okay. Well since the middle of last month, I've noticed substantial enemy units have vanished from the Kraut order of battle in Westphalia. And have you noticed any Kraut armour on our own front since the beginning of December?'

'No sir,' Hardt said, mystified a little by the trend of the conversation.

'So what does that add up to, Hardt?' Koch answered his own question. 'It adds up to this. The Kraut has built a big strategic reserve somewhere along the Western Front, including as many as five hundred panzers. Now is that force going to remain passive, or has Hitler assigned it an active role?' Now Koch sounded like the professor he had once been, Hardt could not help thinking, lecturing a class of bored students on some dreary winter afternoon.

The Colonel rose to his feet and walked over to the big wall map of the Western Front. 'We in Intelligence have attempted to reconstruct the two major Kraut assembly areas for this somewhat mysterious force. One, we figure, is here in the Cologne-Dusseldorf area — *west* of the Rhine. So that one presents no immediate danger, at least for the Third Army. But the other one is further south, in the general area of Gerolstein — here — north of Trier. Now the Krauts are moving the troops in the Cologne-Dusseldorf area by day —'

'Which means they know we'll spot them. So they're no danger.'

'Right in one, Hardt.' Koch beamed at the young Major, with the completely bald head (which had gained him the nickname of 'Hairless Harry' among the men of T-Force behind his back) as if he were a bright student who had just handed in an 'A' grade paper. 'They're the decoys to my way of thinking. But the other group, here at Gerolstein, are moving at night.' 'But sir,' Hardt protested, 'even if the Krauts were preparing to strike, and I hardly think it's likely, then they've scraped the barrel clean. Would they launch a major attack in this kind of weather?' He pointed to the window and the snowflakes drifting down, as if they would never stop again.

Koch chuckled. 'So what are we doing in this kind of weather? We're attacking through the Saar and further north, Hodges' First Army is about to do the same in the Ardennes. Do I need to labour the point any further, Major, eh?'

Hardt held up his hands, as if to ward him off. 'Okay, okay, Colonel, I get the point! You don't need to draw pictures.'

Koch's grin vanished. 'Two days ago, Major Hardt, something happened, which still gives me the creeps. I feel as if I'm suddenly blindfolded and in a dark cellar, trying to find a guy who can see and is armed with a knife and is about to stab me where it hurts, at any minute. But you tell him Black Market.' He waved a pudgy hand at the keen-looking Major.

'*Black Market?*' Hardt echoed puzzled.

The other Major grinned suddenly, showing a mouthful of gleaming white teeth. 'It's the Colonel's little joke, Major Hardt. You see we provide him with information at a pretty high price — Black Market prices, you might say — and under the counter. Like it used to be with Scotch in Old Blighty before D-Day, you remember?' Hardt nodded warily, but he had not really understood.

'I belong to the Signal Intelligence Service, attached to Army HQ. Now it's our job to tap the enemy communications traffic and break whatever material we think might be of interest to Intelligence,' the Major explained. 'Okay, we're usually rushed off our feet. We normally simply don't have enough skilled decoders and operators to take down the volume of material passing from one Kraut unit to another.' He hesitated for a moment. 'Two days ago, however, Major Hardt, the whole goddam German radio system went dead. Not a single squeak from them. Since the Fourteenth of December, the quarter of a million Krauts we estimate are located in the area between Trier and Gerolstein haven't even sent a radio request for more rubbers to be used in the Army cathouses!' Black Market stared across at Hardt almost accusingly.

Abruptly a heavy silence descended upon the big room; there was no sound save the soft swish of the still falling snow and the steady tick of the wall clock, marking the passage of time with metallic inexorability. 'Gentlemen,' Koch broke the silence at last, his mind made up, 'I think it is time that we, Intelligence, and the representatives of long-range reconnaissance and radio intelligence, should go and see the General.'

Hardt nodded his grotesque head slowly in agreement. 'Yes, sir, I think we'd better see General Patton. And quick!'

Sprawled in a big chair, General Patton, the Commander of the US Third Army, his gleaming riding boots muddy-soled from a day in the field with his troops, sipped his favourite 'armoured diesel', an explosive mixture of half a dozen liquors, and listened in silence to each officer. Finally Koch finished his account of the vanished Germans and the details of their sudden radio silence, and waited for Patton's reaction. But Hardt could see the 'Old Man' was tired. It had been a long day — a long winter in fact — and it had taken its toll. Instead of the usual explosive reaction that Hardt knew — and sometimes feared — from the start of the campaign in Europe, six months before, Patton said quietly. 'Well, what do you make of it, Oscar?'

'I don't know what it means when the *Germans* go on radio silence, sir,' Koch answered quickly, happy obviously that the hard-faced, lean, greying General hadn't blown his top, 'But I do know that when *we* place one of our outfits on radio silence, it means they are going to move. And when we move an outfit, more often than not, *it's going into action!*' He emphasized the words firmly.

Patton stopped drinking, his glass poised at his lips. 'Where?'

'It's only an educated guess, General, but for what it's worth, I think it's —' But Colonel Koch never finished his sentence.

At that same moment the door was thrown open without knocking. It was Colonel Harkins, normally so immaculate and contained. But now his Ike jacket was unbuttoned and his face was red and flustered.

The angry comment died on Patton's lips. 'What's up, Paul?' he demanded. 'Where's the goddam fire?'

Harkins pulled himself together hastily. 'Sorry to have to disturb you, sir. But it's the Supreme Commander on the line — and it's bad news!'

Patton put down his glass hastily and seized the phone next to his chair. He pressed the scrambler and rapped. 'Patton — General Eisenhower.'

Hardly daring to breath, the other four officers stared down at Patton and saw immediately that the news must be bad, very bad. The Commanding General's face was growing visibly more grey as he listened to whatever news General Eisenhower had for him from far-off Paris. Finally, Patton said: 'Thanks for the information, you can rely on me to back you right to the hilt. I'll stop my Saar offensive at once. And say, listen Ike — the best of luck!'

Slowly Patton put down the phone. For what seemed a long time he said nothing, his lean hard face as grey and depressed as the weather itself, while his officers stared at him like the characters at the end of the third act of some fourth-rate melodrama, frozen into their absurd postures, waiting for the curtain to go down at last.

Patton took up the armoured diesel and took a sip of the powerful drink with a hand, which Hardt noticed trembled slightly. 'Gentlemen,' he announced hoarsely, 'the Supreme Commander has just informed me that the Krauts hit the First Army's lines in the Ardennes at zero six hundred hours this morning. G-2 Intelligence at Supreme Headquarters has already identified ten Kraut outfits at divisional strength.' He smiled suddenly, but there was no answering light in his pale blue eyes. 'Oscar', he said through his dingy, sawn-off teeth, 'I think you know now where your missing Krauts are at, don't you?'

Morosely Colonel Koch nodded his head in agreement, as from far, far away the first frightening rumble of the new German all-out offensive began to penetrate the suddenly silent room…

CHAPTER 3

As the brass started to file after the Supreme Commander into the bitterly cold squad room of Verdun's *Maginot Caserne*, Major Hardt relaxed from the position of attention and shut the door behind General Patton. The big conference on the new battle in the Ardennes could begin. Now it was his primary concern to get his men under cover after the long, freezing journey across France from Nancy to Verdun. 'Okay Clarry,' he snapped at his Second-in-Command, 1st Lieutenant Clarence van Fleet, whose thin refined face was blue with cold. 'We've got the Old Man here safely. Tell the guys they can take five.' He blew on his frozen fingers. 'Get 'em under cover.'

'Wilco,' the 1st Lieutenant answered in his soft cultivated accent, which befitted the son of a Bostonian millionaire from the 'Hill': an accent that belied the fact that he was a born killer, who was fond of maintaining that "the knife is the most civilized of weapons." 'And believe you me, sir, the boys can use some heat — and perhaps some chow — after that trip.' Van Fleet shivered dramatically, his breath fogging the air grey. 'Jesus H, it was colder than a well digger's ass in those open half-tracks!'

Major Harry Hardt smiled faintly and watched as the handsome 1st Lieutenant, his favourite weapon, a razor-sharp dagger, stuffed down the side of his combat boot, dismissed the frozen T-Force men, who had escorted General Patton from Nancy, expecting trouble round every corner. According to Intelligence, since the big new Kraut offensive had started three days ago, the enemy had dropped hundreds of professional killers by parachute behind the American lines and

Colonel Koch was not taking any chances with old Blood an' Guts' safety.

In spite of their frozen faces and scarlet dripping noses, the 120 men who made up his élite T-Force still looked what they were: a handpicked force of battle-hardened veterans, who were not only tough, but highly skilled in the dangerous business of obtaining long-range intelligence and reconnaissance information from far behind enemy lines. It was no wonder that General Patton called them his 'eyes and ears,' Hardt mused as they walked away stiff-legged, across the white gleaming cobbles of the square towards the inviting warmth of the PX. Yet all the same he wondered why the General had asked for T-Force to escort him to the conference with Eisenhower and the rest of the SHAEF. Why hadn't he used the company of MPs at his HQ?

Puzzled a little, he walked side by side with van Fleet to the Officers' Club, while above them on the grim naked heights, which dominated the drab frontier fortress city, where in 1916 the greatest bloodletting in modern history had taken place, the soft snowflakes began to drift down again. Finally he could keep his thoughts to himself no longer. 'Clarry,' he said slowly, 'what do you think? Why did the Old Man pick us for his escort when we could have been doing much more useful work up front?'

As van Fleet opened the door to the Officers' Club and the thick, noisy fug from inside hit them an almost physical blow in the face, the Second in Command grinned and said softly: 'Can't you guess, sir… Because as soon as the conference over there is finished, Old Blood and Guts is gonna find something — as usual, particularly unpleasant — for T-Force to do.' He wiped the dewdrop from the end of his crimson nose. 'Hell, isn't that why they call us T-Force!'

With an almost angry movement, Major Hardt kicked the door closed behind him and removed his helmet to reveal his pink scalp, 'Yeah, I guess when the shit hits the fan over there, it's gonna be the Tough-Tittie outfit that's at the receiving end of it...'

General Strong, Eisenhower's big Scottish Chief of Intelligence began the conference. Swiftly and confidently he sketched in what had happened on the Ardennes front since the Germans had launched their surprise offensive the previous Saturday. Already Intelligence had identified three German armies on a front of some sixty miles — the Sixth SS Panzer in the north and the Seventh Infantry in the south. But it was the central army, General von Manteuffel's Fifth Panzer which was making the running. It had already chewed up two whole US Divisions, virtually surrounded the key rail and road communications centre at St Vith in Belgium and was beginning to push westwards to the River Meuse, the Germans' primary objective. 'Gentlemen,' he concluded, staring around the assembled generals' pale, set faces, aware — most of them — for the first time just how serious the situation in the Ardennes was, 'the front is fluid and due to the fog, air reconnaissance is impossible.' He shrugged in that un-English way which he had picked up during his years on the Continent. 'We know too little of what is going on up there — it might be worse than we think, it might be better. Thank you,' he sat down suddenly.

Now it was the Supreme Commander's turn. His face was set and pale and the well-known grin, which had endeared him to millions of people all over the western world was absent this grey December afternoon. He looked around his generals and then he said: 'The present situation is to be regarded as one of opportunity for us — and not one of disaster.' He forced a tired, worried smile. 'There will be only cheerful faces at this conference table.'

The ice was broken. As usual Patton was first to react. Eisenhower's remark appealed to his pugnacious nature, although in these last few months he had come to hate Eisenhower — 'the best general the Limeys have', as he was wont to sneer to his cronies behind the Supreme Commander's back. 'Attaboy, Ike!' he snorted. 'Hell, let's have the guts to let the sons of bitches go all the way to Paris! Then we'll really cut 'em off and show 'em up!'

Even Bradley, Patton's Chief, managed a slow, leathery smile, though he was not much given to humour this day when he had just learned that his 'calculated risk' of keeping the sixty-mile front in the Ardennes manned by four weak divisions had not paid off.

'Okay, Georgie,' Eisenhower said. 'Let's not give General de Gaulle a heart attack with suggestions like that. Now this is what I want you to do. I want you to go to Luxembourg and take charge of the battle, making a strong counter-attack with at least six divisions.'

'Yessir,' Patton snapped, though he didn't have the least idea of how he could manage to release six divisions from his front in the Saar.

'Now when can you start, Georgie?'

'As soon as you're through with me,' Patton answered promptly.

Eisenhower frowned. Around the table senior officers shifted uneasily in their seats at Patton's typical rashness. A British general guffawed out loud and told himself — typical Yankee big mouthed brashness. Patton would have to free his divisions from the line and swinging them right around, launch them in thousands of vehicles, hundreds of miles down icy, enemy-held roads right into the southern flank of the German attack. It seemed an impossible undertaking.

'What do you mean?' Eisenhower snapped.

'I left my household in Nancy in perfect order before I came here,' Patton replied, 'and can go to Luxembourg right away, sir, straight from here.'

With a nod, Eisenhower absorbed the information. 'And when will you be able to attack?'

'*The morning of December 22nd, sir!*' Patton said, and seizing the chance to dampen the Supreme Commander's enthusiasm a bit, 'but with *three* divisions.'

The reaction to Patton's deadline was electric. There was a stir, a shuffling of feet. Some of the men present had known Patton for many a year. They knew his boastfulness, but also his boldness. Perhaps he might be able to pull it off! Others were less convinced; their faces showed their scepticism.

Eisenhower obviously belonged to the second group. He lost his temper suddenly. 'Don't be fatuous, George,' he rapped sternly.

Patton remained cool, perhaps the only one in the room to do so. 'This has nothing to do with being fatuous,' he said calmly. 'I've made my arrangements and my staff are working like beavers at this very moment to shape them up.' Swiftly he explained his tentative plan and added, 'I'm positive I can make a strong attack on the 22nd, but only with *three* divisions, the 26th and 80th Infantry and my Fourth Armoured. I can't attack with more until some days later, but I'm determined to attack on the 22nd with what I've got because if I wait I lose surprise.' Suddenly he turned to his boss, General Bradley, 'Brad, this time the Kraut has stuck his head in a meat grinder. And this time *I've* got hold of the goddam handle !' He grinned. 'We've got him. by the short and curlies!'

With that the meeting broke up and the brass began to move to the door. There Eisenhower raised a finger in warning. 'Remember, Georgie, the advance has to be methodical — sure!'

Patton removed the big, expensive Havana from his mouth and grinned, obviously very pleased with the effect he had had on the vital conference. 'I'll be in Bastogne before Christmas, sir.'

Patton waited till the brass had driven off back to their headquarters in Paris and Luxembourg; then he started to rap out orders, the grin gone from his face. 'Paul,' he snapped at a frozen Colonel Harkins, 'telephone my HQ. Give them the code number' — he was referring to the code number of the new operation he had worked out with his staff during the last two days — 'and tell them to get started. Then get back to Nancy yourself as soon as you can. You know what to do?'

'Yessir,' Harkins barked, his breath a white cloud on the freezing air, and doubled away to find the nearest telephone.

'Codman,' he called to his senior aide, 'get the auto round here at the double. Tell the driver we're starting for Luxembourg in five minutes.'

'But sir,' Codman protested. 'You haven't got a pair of pyjamas or even a toothbrush with you —'

'So what!' Patton broke in, 'What the goddam hell! Do you think I'm gonna stab the Krauts to death with my toothbrush? Away with you, Charley!'

Codman went.

Finally Patton turned to the waiting Major Hardt. He looked at the Major for a brief moment and liked what he saw. Hardt was a younger version of himself — from the gleaming brass sabres of the Regular Cavalry on his immaculate Ike jacket down to the perfectly tailored white whipcord breeches tucked into gleaming custom-made riding boots. A West Pointer from head to toe, just like himself. The sight gave him confidence in the success of the mission he was going to assign to the T-Force Commander; if anyone could pull it off, it would be Major Hardt.

'Listen son, I've got a dilly for you,' he said softly, almost emotionally. He stared at the Major in silence.

'Sir?'

From the direction of the PX, Hardt could hear Limey's raucous voice bellowing. *'Now this is number one and he's got her on the run, roll me over in the clover and do it agen!'*

'You know the big picture by now, don't you? The Krauts are pretty deep in 1st Army's territory and are barrelling for the Meuse. The major threat, of course, is von Manteuffel's Fifth Panzer Army. He's already got St Vith and my guess is that he's well on his way for the next major road centre on the way to the Meuse-Bastogne. Okay?'

Hardt nodded his understanding.

'In this kind of weather a tank army commander needs those Belgian roads and road centres like a wino needs his pint of rotgut. So, Hardt,' Patton's voice hardened, 'I've got to get Bastogne before Manteuffel does. It's the one way of stopping him getting to the Meuse.'

'I see, sir,' Hardt made it easy for the Old Man. 'And T-Force's mission?'

'Up there in Belgium, we're fighting in the dark. All I know is that one whole Kraut army is heading like a bat outa hell for Bastogne. Hardt, you've got to plough through that Army and find a route for my Fourth Armoured to follow as soon as I get it to its start-line on the 22nd. Listen son,' abruptly Patton was a pleading, old man, 'find me that route, please... *It's Bastogne or bust by Christmas...'*

CHAPTER 4

'*Heaven, arse and twine,*' the little General, whose coat and hat looked too big for him, cursed angrily to his amused companion, 'where the devil are those fine paras of yours going now, Steiner?' He focused his glasses on the blue-clad figures of the 5th Parachute Division, who were now straggling through the snow towards the town of Wiltz like a crowd of sloppy schoolchildren. 'Don't they know they're supposed to bypass the damned place, not take it?'

The tall parachute Major, with the tough cleft chin and the faded blue, cynical eyes, shrugged easily. Harmut Steiner had long given up worrying about the activities of large-scale formations. After five years of war, he detested the great amorphous mass of the conventional formations; he was only at home with a handful of well-trained, determined men who like himself believed that boldness and dash counted; not numbers. 'With your permission, General von Manteuffel, what can you expect from Fat Hermann's present to the Führer for the offensive? Up to a couple of months ago they were clerks, cooks, any kind of bottlewasher. Not one of them is a trained para. Now it's getting close to evening, so what do they do? Orders or not, they head for the nearest houses where they can tuck themselves into nice warm beds for the night.' He shrugged once again. 'They're what we call Christmas tree soldiers!'

The Fifth Panzer Army's Commander lowered his glasses and grinned. Then his birdlike face hardened again. Somewhere a lone American mortar had opened up. A sudden brown hole like the work of some gigantic mole had appeared in the surface of the snow. The young paras of the Fifth Division were scattering wildly, as if the whole weight of the American Army's artillery were about to descend upon them. 'Great God and all his triangles,' he cursed, 'they'll never get round Wiltz this day if they go on like that! How in three devils' name does the Führer ever expect me to get to the Meuse with units like that! *Ach, das ist doch zum Kotzen!*'

Abruptly he dismissed the rabble digging in wildly below, as if they were intent on getting to Australia. He turned his hard, piercing gaze on the tall Para Major and liked what he saw. Steiner bore the black and white *Kreta* armband which indicated that he was one of the few survivors of the great paradrop on Crete in '41; and his broad chest was covered in decorations from the Knight's Cross to the Wound Medal in Silver, which meant that he had been hit six times. The Major had obviously seen his share of action in these last five terrible years. 'Steiner,' he snapped, 'I've got a mission for you, and your Independent Para Company.'

'*Sir!*' Steiner's lazy grin vanished instantly. The prospect of getting away from the Division obviously pleased him. 'What is it?'

'This.' With his stick, von Manteuffel traced a line in the snow. 'The River Meuse,' he announced, 'the only major barrier between the Fifth Panzer Army and its objective — Brussels. Now, as you know, our armour is going to be mainly road-bound in this kind of weather — and the Ardennes is poorly supplied with roads.'

Steiner nodded his understanding but said nothing. Down below the lone American mortar had stopped firing, but still the green young soldiers of the 5th Para Division had not begun to move out of their holes.

'As a result the road centres are of vital importance to us. St Vith is nearly ours — it will fall any hour now. But there is still Bastogne between us and the Meuse. In enemy hands the place could influence all our movements to the west, damage our supply system and tie up considerable German forces. It is essential we capture it at once before the *Amis* do —'

'You mean, sir, that they are moving troops up there? I thought they didn't have any reserves in the Ardennes? That is why the Führer, in his infinite wisdom,' Steiner allowed himself a smile, 'picked the area for this offensive.' Von Manteuffel looked at Steiner coldly. 'Major,' he snapped, 'I don't want you to talk like that of the Führer in my presence! Keep your opinion of the greatest captain of all times to yourself. I think it will be better for you to do so.'

'At your service, General,' Steiner answered, in no way frighttened. He knew that von Manteuffel, the aristocratic ex-cavalry officer and gentleman jockey, held the same opinion as himself about the man he called 'the Bohemian Corporal' behind his back contemptuously. The General was just trying to warn him, that was all. 'I thank you for the advice.' 'Good, then let's get on with it. The Americans don't have any reserves in the Ardennes. But yesterday we picked up their radio message from France and England, altering the 101st Airborne Division to move up from France to Bastogne. Obviously Eisenhower is having to scrape the barrel if he intends to use paratroopers for such a ground role. Trained paras are a costly item to throw away as ordinary stubble hoppers.' He drew another line from the west in the snow. 'So we have the American paratroopers coming from Northern France and my own Panzer Lehr Division and the Second Panzer moving in from the East — here. Now I don't doubt that my tankers will get to Bastogne. It is not the paratroopers

I'm worried about. If they're anything like that bunch down there,' he indicated the men of the Fifth, who were now beginning to move out of their holes cautiously and recommence their advances towards Wiltz, 'we'll be in Bastogne having our Christmas goose by the time they arrive. *No*, my problem lies here to the south.' He drew a fourth line in the snow. 'Luxembourg and the Saar.'

'Why there, sir?' Steiner asked curiously, wondering where he and his Company fitted into all this,

'Because my dear Steiner, that is where General George Patton junior is located.'

'The *Ami* Cowboy General!' Steiner breathed.

'Yes, the Cowboy General. But we must not underestimate him. In spite of his loud-mouthed behaviour he is a cunning fox for an American. And he is bold. They tell me in intelligence that he is an old man — sixty. Such men have little to lose, save their lives.' General von Manteuffel, nearly twenty years Patton's junior, pursed his lips thoughtfully. 'They have lost their teeth, they have lost their potency too, most of them. They have lost the vanities of youth. Already they have one foot in the grave. *But*,' he raised his stick in the air warningly, 'they still have one dream.'

'And that is, sir?' Steiner asked, half-amused, half-intrigued at this attempt by one general to analyse the attitudes of another one.

'Immortality!'

'What?'

'Oh, yes, Steiner, they want to go down in the history books — *at any cost*! Casualties don't worry them, they are half-dead themselves any way. Why should they worry about the fates of young men? So! They become bolder than they were when they were forty. They will attack and attack, and attack once again, as long as those attacks bring them glory — and immortality. Such a man is our Cowboy General. Thus I fear him.'

'But why, sir?' Steiner protested. 'What can he do? After all, the bulk of his Third Army is located in the Saar.'

'I know what he will do. The Saar will win him no laurels. A cowboy like Patton finds no pleasure in attacking a fortified line such as our West Wall. No, he will offer his services to attack my left flank. That is the kind of fluid, fast-moving warfare that he likes. But that will not be enough for him. He will have to concentrate his attack on some objective which will ensure him the headlines. Something already fixed in the petty minds of those armchair warriors back in his own country beyond the Big Ocean.'

'St Vith or Bastogne?' Steiner exclaimed eagerly, realising now what the diminutive General was getting at.

'Not St Vith because our Cowboy General is realistic enough to know that he'd never make it. No, *Bastogne* — and, my dear Steiner, unlike those paratroopers in Northern France, he has armour at his disposal, a lot of it.'

Von Manteuffel let the information sink in. Then he took his stick and drew a wavy line in the snow. 'The River Sure, Steiner,' he explained, 'running from the German frontier through Luxembourg and below Bastogne. All the approach roads, major and minor, to the city must cross that river. You understand?' 'Yessir.' Already it was beginning to dawn on Steiner what his objective was going to be.

'So if my prognosis is correct and our famous Cowboy General does attack my flank, with Bastogne as his objective, he will have to cross that river. Now, of course, right from the start I anticipated some sort of an attack on my flank. Hence the Fifth Para Division. They were to be the infantry which would protect me from being caught — if you will forgive the phrase — with my drawers down. But,' he indicated the paras down below, already beginning to loot the first houses in Wiltz, 'you can see the type of troops they are. They will get to the Sure eventually, but the question is *when*? And with that Cowboy General now breathing down my neck, I can't afford to takes chances. That is why I asked Heilmann for you.'

Steiner tensed slightly, although his facial expression did not change. This was it!

'Your company, I believe, is the only one in the Division which is fully jump-trained?'

'Yessir.'

'So you have one hundred and fifty trained paras at your disposal. Now there are four Junkers transports waiting for you at the emergency landing strip outside Bitburg. You will proceed there with your company immediately you leave me, divide them into three major sections and drop them at the major bridges crossing the River Sure. My Intelligence Chief will brief you more fully in the car on your way back to Bitburg.'

Steiner nodded his understanding and looked up at the sky. It was leaden and ominous with further snow. 'Heaven is hanging full of violins, sir,' he said mildly, not wanting to appear too afraid, too hesitant.

'What is that supposed to mean, Steiner?' von Manteuffel snapped.

'A night jump is bad enough, sir. But it looks as if it's going to snow too. That makes it even tougher. It's no fun going out for a little walk in the air even in the best of weather, you know, sir.'

Von Manteuffel shrugged and turned up the fur collar of his greatcoat, as if the interview were finished for him. 'All I know,

Steiner, is that your vaunted paras must stop the Cowboy's lead troops until the rest of that rabble down there come up. If you're going make an omelette, you've got to crack eggs. After five years of war, Steiner, you ought to know that now.' He tucked his stick under his arm and prepared to go. On the road, his driver began to rev the Mercedes' engine. 'Steiner, I want that Cowboy General stopped before he gets even within sniffing distance of Bastogne!'

Suddenly Major Hartmut Steiner grinned, his fears forgotten now. General von Manteuffel was no different from the American Cowboy either, he wanted immortality too. As the Fifth Panzer Army Commander started to walk to his car, he flung him an immaculate salute and bellowed at the top of his voice, as if he were a young recruit back at the training centre at Stendhal, 'Major Steiner, 1st Independent Para Company respectfully reports that he will execute plan according to instructions, *Herr General!*'

The race for Bastogne was on...

PART TWO: INDIAN COUNTRY

'Major, the Krauts know you're coming. They'll be waiting for you up in that goddam Indian country!' —

General Sibert to Major Hardt, Dec 19-20th, 1944.

CHAPTER 1

The T-Force column started to rumble into Luxembourg City just before dark on the 19th. But in spite of the icy wind blowing across the hills on which the capital of the tiny Principality was located, the cobbled streets were crowded. Everywhere there were groups of silent, anxious, shabby civilians watching the long convoys of American vehicles, filled with dirty, exhausted GIs, retreating from the front, heading for the south and safety. Now the Old Glory flags, the welcoming banners, the signs reading 'English Spoken Here', the pictures in windows of Roosevelt and Churchill had disappeared overnight. And as the T-Force vehicles began to roll down the Rue de Gare towards the Alpha Hotel, Bradley's HQ, the civilians standing on the pavements on both sides did not doff their caps as a sign of respect to their 'liberators', as they had done instinctively only a few days before. Already they could hear the rumble of German artillery a matter of a few miles away; the *Wehrmacht was* coming back as they had always promised they would and soon there would be a reckoning with those who had sided with the Americans during their three-month stay in the capital. The Luxembourgers were playing it safe!

It seemed that Bradley's staff were doing the same. As 'Old Baldy' Hardt's command half-track came to a halt at the big, dark-coloured Hotel Alpha opposite the station, the tired T-Force men could see the HQ clerks staggering out, arms full of secret papers, carrying them to the waiting jeeps and trucks, engines running, tanks fully gassed up, ready to take off at the first sign of a German. Limey nudged Triggerman. 'What do you say to that, old lad?' he cracked. 'Looks as if you Yanks here have got a bad case of the wind-up!'

'Aw go and crap in ya cap!' the sour-faced, ex-Mafia 'soldier' snarled. 'What do you expect from a bunch of lace drawer canteen commandos like that!' He spat drily onto the frozen pavement. 'They wet their skivvies when the First Shirt speaks rough to them!'

Limey laughed, but there was no answering light in his smart, Cockney eyes. He had seen it all before, back when he'd been in Africa before he had deserted from the Eighth Army. One little thing and the whole group of sweating anxious bespectacled clerks and white-helmeted MP guards, their fingers crooked nervously around the triggers of their carbines, would bolt like a bunch of frightened rabbits.

Big Red seemed to think the same, for as Major Hardt and Lieutenant van Fleet dropped stiffly out of the half-track to go inside, he raised his voice and cried. 'Okay, you guys, take five! But I don't want any of youse goofing off. If yer want to piss, yer can go inside to the latrine. But no dames and no booze. Stand by yer vehicles and hold on to yer weapons! Drivers keep yer engines running!' He paused momentarily and looked down contemptuously at a fat sweating clerk, struggling out under the weight of his bedroll and barracks bag, the lead of his pet dog clutched between his teeth, while the little mongrel barked excitedly around his heels. ''Cos when the Krauts come, they're gonna go through this little lot like a dose of senna through a fat whore!'

Grinning, the two T-Force officers showed their ETO cards to the guards and passed into the lounge thronged with excited, elegant staff officers discussing the latest news from the front. They pushed their way to the former reception desk, now manned by a Tech Sergeant, one cigar, in his mouth, another stuck behind his ear in reserve. 'Yeah?' he grunted without looking up, intent on the *Stars and Stripes* crossword.

'Stick a "sir" on that, sergeant!' Hardt ordered, angered by everything he had seen since they had arrived at Bradley's HQ.

The Tech Sergeant looked up slowly and then suddenly his eyes brightened. He whipped the cigar out of his mouth suddenly. 'Gee whiz, *sir*, why didn't you say you was the Third Army, *sir*, instead of this —' he caught himself just in time. 'What can I do for you, *sir*?'

'The G-2 is expecting us, I believe,' Hardt answered, amused at the way the NCO had reacted to the sight of his Third Army patch. Obviously he thought they were the Seventh Cavalry, come to rescue the HQ from the nasty Germans. The Tech Sergeant thrust in the telephone lead with a flourish. 'I'll call General Sibert's office straightaway, *sir*! Just one leetle moment, *sir*!'

General Sibert, Bradley's smooth-faced, young-looking Chief of Intelligence, rapped his West Point class ring against the big map of Luxembourg and Belgium on the rear wall of his office and said almost angrily, 'Gentlemen, that out there is Indian country, as far as G-2 is concerned. Goddam, lousy Indian country!'

Van Fleet flashed Hardt a dismayed look. Even the brass here in Luxembourg seemed to be infected by the defeatist mood. Hardt ignored the look. 'What do you mean exactly, sir?' he ventured slowly.

'I mean, Major,' Sibert replied, controlling himself with difficulty. 'We in Intelligence don't know the goddam Sam Hill what is going on up there at the front in Belgium! Kraut saboteurs and the local yokels working with them have cut our lines everywhere, and all we can get from that rabble of deserters and stragglers down there,' he indicated a fresh column of dispirited, unshaven GIs heading south, down below, 'is that the line is bugging out all over. But one thing is for sure — the Krauts are up there somewhere.'

'We kinda anticipated that,' Hardt answered gently. Sibert smiled suddenly. 'Okay, okay, Major, you don't need to draw me a picture. I know I'm rambling on like a goddam little old lady. But it's the darn uncertainty. If we only had some hard intelligence on what is really going on up there in Belgium instead of scuttlebutt and latrine rumours.' He shrugged. 'But we haven't, so that's that.'

'What do you suggest for T-Force then, sir?' Hardt ventured. 'You know our mission. How are we to accomplish it?'

'Okay,' Sibert turned to the big map again. 'As you can see the terrain is pretty rugged. These corridors, cut by the rivers Sure and Wiltz,' he traced the lines on the map, 'form pretty effective barriers against any motorized advance. And the entire area is criss-crossed with rivers and streams. Now there are seven entrant roads into Bastogne itself — hence the importance of the place. Now two of those roads come into question for your people. The main highway from Lux through Arlon — here — here — and on through Martelange to Bastogne. Then the second-grade road via Ettelbruck — here. Now you can bet your bottom dollar, Major, if the Krauts are going to establish a blocking position anywhere, it's gonna be on that main highway through Arlon.' Hardt nodded his agreement. 'But what about the Ettelbruck road, sir? There's the Sure at Bourscheid. If they could get hold of the bridge there —'

Sibert was quicker than Hardt. 'Yeah, yeah, I know what you mean, Major. But that's why the Ettelbruck road is your best bet if the Kraut gets to the Sure before you. You can always turn off the main road, here, at Eschdorf, work your way to the main Arlon highway to Martelange and swinging westwards, come in via Neufchâteau, which according to the last information I have was still in our hands.' He sighed deeply, as if everything were a little too much for him. 'And it goddam still better be because it's the goddam Eighth Corps Commander's new HQ!' he added.

The two T-Force officers stared at the big map hard. There were the brown contours of heights and the blue of streams everywhere. As Sibert had said himself it was pretty rugged country; but now with the addition of the new snow, it would be hell. 'Sir,' Hardt broke the heavy silence, disturbed only by the steady rumble of the convoys from the front, fleeing southwards.

'Yes?'

'What about the ground on both sides of the roads, sir? I mean, if we're forced off them into the fields with our armour, would the ground support us?'

Sibert shook his head miserably. 'No deal, Major,' he answered. 'After Mersch — there — you start running into what the local yokels call the Luxembourg Switzerland. What they mean —'

But General Sibert never did explain what the Luxembourg Switzerland was. In that same instant his words were cut short dramatically by the harsh metallic chatter of shellfire. The windows of his office shattered into a gleaming spider's web of broken glass as 20mm shells stitched a deadly pattern across the big map. Icy air streamed in, bringing with it the thin scream of the air-raid sirens and the sudden angry fire of T-Force 50-calibre machineguns down below.

'Kraut Messerschmitt's!' van Fleet yelled urgently and flung himself on the glass-littered floor as the four Me 109s came barrelling in once again. Lined abreast, they zoomed in at rooftop height just above the station cupola, cannon blazing an angry violet. At a rate of a thousand rounds a minute, the shells tore the front of the hotel HQ apart. The noise was ear-splitting, the air full of the harsh biting odour of cordite. Hardt flung himself across the room to the window and beat out the remaining glass with his helmet. He was just in time to catch a glimpse of the last plane's great black-and-white iron cross as it tore almost vertically into the grey leaden sky, chased by angry white tracers from the T-Force column. He cupped his hands around his mouth against the racket. 'Get the hell outa those vehicles!' he bellowed. 'You're sitting ducks down here!'

But Big Red and Triggerman crouched behind Old Baldy's machinegun were not listening. They were already swinging the gun round, feet stumbling over the cartridges which littered the deck everywhere, bringing it to bear on the lead Messerschmitt. The Germans were coming into attack once again!

'*Look out*!' Hardt yelled desperately.

Next instant he was swamped by the roar of the Messerschmitt's engine. Cannon chattered viciously. Shells snaked through the air, trailing fiery red trails behind them. The whole building seemed to shake under the impact. Automatically Hardt opened his mouth to prevent his ear drums being split by the detonations. At the other window Sibert and van Fleet had drawn their forty-fives and were firing wildly at the great light-blue belly of the Messerschmitt. To no avail! It sailed beyond the roof unharmed. The next plane came roaring in at 400 mph. One of the HQ trucks was hit. Next instant it went up in flames, as its gas tank exploded. The fat clerk threw out the little dog before the flames enveloped him. It ran off yelping. The burning truck acted as a spur for the third Messerschmitt. The pilot, obviously intent on a kill too, lowered his undercarriage and tilted his yellow-painted nose slightly. In this manner he could slow up the fighter. For a moment he seemed to hover over the burning station like a sinister great hawk, while he took careful aim.

It was the chance that a crimson-faced Red and a sweating, cursing Triggerman had been waiting for. Frantically they swung the machinegun round. Just as the pilot pressed the button which would activate the eight wing cannon, Big Red pulled the 50-calibre's trigger. The machinegun chattered crazily. White tracer cut through the grey air like a flight of angry bees. The slugs caught the plane right in the engine. The prop flew apart. A thick white stream of glycol poured from the stricken engine. Desperately the pilot threw back the shattered canopy, as the Messerschmitt started to break up. Big Red had no mercy. He pressed the trigger again. The vicious burst caught the pilot squarely across the chest. He slumped across the canopy in the same moment that the plane exploded. As the Messerschmitt disintegrated in a blinding flash of light, Hardt just caught a glimpse of the pilot's body, revolving through the brilliant glare like a diver doing a somersault. It was followed by a small dark object racing through the crazy turbulence at a frantic speed. It was the German pilot's head!

'I just don't believe it,' Sibert gasped, dusting the plaster dust from his knees, as below the ambulance sirens wailed and the wounded groaned pitifully, 'I goddam just don't believe it!'

Hardt, satisfied that none of his men had been hurt, formed a victory O with his thumb and forefinger and winked at a triumphant Big Red, before turning to face the pale-faced General. 'How do you mean, sir?' he queried.

'How do I mean? Shoot, there hasn't been a Kraut plane around Lux City for the last three months! Safer than Piccadilly Circus in the blackout, the HQ doughs maintain. Last air-raid shelter we had here in the Alpha was turned into the top-three graders club last month. So what the Sam Hill are the Krauts doing, running a tip and run raid on Lux for, when they need every goddam kite they've got — and they haven't got that many — up front, eh?'

Thirty minutes later, just before Hardt was about to leave the HQ and set off on his mission into the unknown, General Sibert's question was answered. One of Sibert's junior officers, his face pale and his hands covered in a red liquid which looked suspiciously like blood, was ushered into the room by the Deputy Chief of Intelligence, a Colonel. 'Sir,' he indicated the young man, 'Perkins here has something, I think.'

'Yes, Perkins?' Sibert snapped.

The young officer's lips moved but no words came out.

'For God's sake, Perkins,' Sibert urged, 'speak up, man, or shut up!'

'This … this, sir,' the other man finally managed to get out the words. 'We found it … on the body.' With a hand that trembled violently, he thrust a blood-stained map at the General. 'The map was tucked in the pilot's coverall pocket,' the Colonel explained. 'In the left leg which was shorn off by the force of impact. Perkins here was the first to find it … it kind of shook him.'

'Yes, I can see that all right,' Sibert snapped. 'For God's sake, take him down to the bar and give him a swift slug of something strong before he keels right over!'

When the two of them had departed, Sibert unfolded the sticky, damp map carefully and stared at it thoughtfully, while Hardt and van Fleet watched his stern face for some sort of reaction, wondering what could be so important about the dead pilot's map.

Finally Sibert spoke. 'Come and have a look at this, the two of you,' he commanded.

Slowly they walked across the big room, boots crunching over the glass debris. Together they stared at the blood-stained map in the hissing white glare of the Coleman lamp.

'It's a flight map,' Sibert explained. 'The kind of thing artillery spotters or fighter pilots might use for cross-country hops. You see, they can balance it on their knees, and follow their route, fold by fold, with the main features outlined in thick red ink, raised off the paper so that they could even trace the features in the dark with the tips of their fingers.'

The two officers nodded their understanding. 'Now you can follow the dead pilot's route easily enough — from the Buechel field up on the Moselle, down the river as far as Wasserbillig and then due west to Lux City —'

'Yessir, I can see that,' Hardt said hastily. Down below the T-Force drivers were gunning their cold engines, eager to be on their way; time was running out. 'But what is the importance of the map?'

'This!' Sibert poked a neatly manicured index finger at the centre of Luxembourg City on the map. 'Look at that red circle. Do you know what it is?' He answered his own question. 'It's the Hotel Alpha. *Here*!,' he rapped. 'The Krauts put in that raid in order to knock this HQ out because they know that this is the place from where General Patton is going to command the attack north to Bastogne.' He hesitated momentarily and looked at Hardt with a set face. 'Major, the Krauts know you're coming. *They'll be waiting for you...*'

CHAPTER 2

But General Sibert was not quite right in his guess about the purpose of the tip and run raid on Luxembourg City. It was not to knock out Bradley's HQ, but to draw attention away from the four ancient Junkers transports ploughing their way steadily westwards that snowy night; and it had been Major Steiner's idea.

Now Steiner's First Independent Para Company was preparing for their jump over the blacked-out terrain below. Up ahead the dull red warning light was already beginning to glow and the dispatcher was fumbling with the exit door. Steiner looked at the two lines of men who would follow him out into the night to bar the Ettelbruck-Bastogne road. Underneath their rimless helmets the men's faces looked pale and set, but there was no fear in their eyes. They were his veterans. As always just before a combat jump, their minds would be racing with the same overwhelming questions. Will I be hurt?... Will the *Amis* fire upon us while we're hanging helplessly in mid-air?... *What if my chute doesn't open*? But their tough, battle-hardened faces revealed none of the doubts plaguing them at this moment.

'Todt,' he cried, above the roar of the Junkers' three engines, to the broken-nosed Sergeant Major sitting next to him, who like himself bore the *Kreta* armband, 'Tell 'em to make one last inspection of the chute! What do we need a chute for,' Todt roared back with his usual hoary-old joke on such occasions, 'our boot soles are thick enough, aren't they, sir?'

'Get on with it, Todt,' Steiner replied, smiling in spite of his inner tension. 'I'm going to check with the captain.'

While Steiner stumbled forward to the cockpit, Todt ordered the paras to check their new experimental parachute, copied from a captured Russian model, which because of its triangular shape was supposed to be oscillation-free.

'Well?' Steiner demanded of the grey-helmeted pilot, 'have the other planes dumped their loads?'

The pilot handed over the transport to his co-pilot and rubbed his strained, red-rimmed eyes. 'They've just signalled they have. But in this weather, God knows where they are. Great crap on the Christmas tree!', he explained wearily, 'that snow is hitting us like flak. Can't see a shitty thing!' He looked up at Steiner suddenly, 'Do you really want to go through with this, Major? You've got a good excuse for turning back — the wind's shittingly well beginning to rise now too!'

Steiner shook his head and grinned, though he had never felt more serious. 'No, Captain,' he answered. 'This'll be just like a training jump for my boys. That hairy-arsed lot of old bastards back there don't worry about such things as snow and a bit of wind.'

The pilot shrugged. 'Be it on your own head, Major. But I'll bring the plane down to minimum jumping height. That'll give you the best chance of not being dispersed too much by the wind.'

'A good idea,' Steiner agreed, though he didn't add that a low drop height would also ensure they might have a nice old collection of twisted ankles and broken legs. 'Make it three-fifty metres.'

'*Einverstanden!*'

Three minutes later the paras were strapped to their static lines, arranged in two files behind Major Steiner, poised at the door, the icy wind, mixed with flakes of snow, whipping at his coveralls.

Next to the jumpmaster, the green light began to blink urgently. 'Ready, sir?' the sergeant bellowed.

Behind Steiner, Todt took his big paw off the Major's shoulder. 'Ready!'

The jumpmaster's hand slapped down hard on Steiner's back. '*Go!*'

Major Steiner jumped into the whirling white world of the night. The weight of his pack and chute seemed to snatch him out of the Junkers like a great invisible hand. He caught a glimpse of the plane's black rump and then he was dropping at a terrifying speed. Would the damn chute never open? Then there was a loud crack and the triangle of white billowed free above him. A tug at his shoulders and he was heading straight for the ground. He twisted his helmeted head upwards and looked for the rest of his force. But there was nothing to be seen through the driving snow. He shrugged and concentrated on his own drop; now it would be every man for himself. Suddenly a violent gust of wind caught him. Everything else was forgotten as he felt himself being driven to the west at a tremendous speed. The triangular shaped parachute had not been designed to cope with such wind speed. Cursing furiously, Major Steiner tugged at the shroud lines, fighting the chute. A snow-covered forest rushed up to meet him. Instinctively he recalled from his study of the drop zone map that there had been no wood within five kilometres of the place; he was well off course. But there was no time to worry about that now.

The spiked firs were everywhere. He tensed, knees drawn up to protect himself.

Too late! The howling wind carried him right into the forest. Twigs slashed against his face cruelly. He yelped with pain as a branch dug hard into his ribs. Abruptly his nostrils were assailed by the heavy scent of resin. Another branch snapped back and hit him a vicious blow across the face. For an instant Steiner blacked out. When he came to again, the trees had gone and he was hurtling to a stop in the middle of an open field.

He hit the frozen, snow-covered ground hard, rolling over only at the last moment to take some of the impact away. For one long moment he lay there paralysed, listening to the howl of the wind and his own harsh breathing. Then he pulled himself together. Swiftly he rose to his feet. Before the chute could belly out in the wind, he pressed the two release buttons on his chest. With fingers that trembled violently, he unstrapped his knee pads. He dropped them in the snow carelessly; there was no time to bury them now. Hastily he clicked the safety catch off his machine pistol and stood upright, his head turned right into the wind so that he could hear better. But there was no sound but its howl. Major Hartmut Steiner, CO of the 121st Independent Para Company was alone!

By dawn Steiner had collected Todt, another sergeant with a twisted ankle, and eighteen men, one of whom had broken his arm during the jump. But injured or not, all of them were frozen and exhausted by their long struggle to find their comrades through the driving snow. Shivering with cold, smoking cigarettes cautiously behind cupped frozen hands, they were now hidden in a snowy copse close by a narrow cobbled road, while their CO and Todt surveyed their position.

'What do you make of it, Todt?' Steiner asked a little helplessly as his strained eyes failed to penetrate the grey, snow-filled gloom ahead up the road.

'Situation normal, sir,' Todt answered easily, as if they were on a training exercise. 'The usual shitty mess!'

'You can say that again. Heaven, arse and twine!' he exclaimed with sudden impotent anger. 'If I only knew where we were, Todt!'

'Don't take it to heart, sir,' Todt answered, his rough voice softened. 'It's not your fault, sir. Remember what a balls up Crete was in '41? This is a picnic in comparison.'

'Yes, I suppose you're right.' Steiner flashed a quick glance at the green-glowing dial of the compass strapped to his wrist. 'All right, we can't hang around here much longer, waiting till the *Amis* round us up or this damn cold freezes our outside plumbing up for good. We'd better get moving.'

Todt dropped his cigarette and ground it out carefully in the hissing snow. 'Your orders, Major?' he rapped.

'We march eastwards along this road in two files at fifty metres distance. Somewhere along the line we must come to a signpost, then we can orientate ourselves and head south to the River Sure.'

'At your command, sir,' Todt answered, as if it were the most natural thing on earth to attempt to carry out their original plan under such terrible conditions with only a handful of beaten, exhausted men at their disposal. 'All right, you happy heroes, you,' he called softly to the paras. 'On yer feet and air your arses — we're on our way!'

Wearily the paras began to plod through the deep snow of the road to the east.

The lead half-track caught the paras completely by surprise. Suddenly it loomed up out of the driving snow and skidded to a halt, machinegun trained on them. Horrified, Steiner began to raise his frozen hands; there was no other way out. But he never completed that final gesture. Suddenly a harsh Prussian voice demanded: 'What in three devils' name are you paras doing here?'

Steiner breathed out a sigh of heartfelt relief. They had bumped into the point of a German armoured column, for now he could see the line of snow-covered Panthers lined up behind the half-track! He lowered his hands and walked swiftly to the man who had asked the question. He caught a glimpse of a thin face, heavy-lensed glasses, a long leather coat, surmounted by the gold epaulettes of a general and clicked to attention. He had recognised the face. He was in the presence of the legendary Lt. General Fritz Bayerlein, Rommel's onetime Chief of Staff in the desert, now the commander of the élite Panzer Lehr Division. In awkward broken phrases, shaken by the sudden meeting with one of the Reich's most legendary commanders out here in the middle of nowhere, he explained his mission.

Bayerlein listened attentively, while behind him the battery of radios in the command half-track chattered continually. When Steiner was finished, he said with supreme confidence, 'Don't worry, Major. We'll be in Bastogne long before the *Amis*, And even if we do bump into the advance guard of their 101st Airborne Division coming up from France, we're armour and they're armed with only the lightest of infantry weapons.' He shrugged easily. 'It would be a massacre.'

'But they're paras, sir,' Steiner objected.

Bayerlein gave him a toothy smile. '*Paras*, eh?' he echoed. 'I've always thought you chaps were highly overrated. Now then, do you want to come along with my column?'

'No sir,' Steiner snapped. 'We'll go it alone, if it's all right with you?'

'Naturally it's all right with me.' Bayerlein turned to his driver. 'Fritz, take her away. *Forward*!'

The frozen driver of the half-track needed no further urging. He rammed home first gear and let out the clutch. Steiner and Todt stepped out of the way hastily, as the big command half-track started to rattle forward, followed by the Panthers.

'*Overrated*!' Todt growled, rubbing his broken nose, as tank after tank rolled by them heading for Mageret, a village ten kilometres west of Bastogne. 'He should have been with us at Eben-Emael or Crete or even Cassino last year, then he'd have a bit more respect for the paras.'

'But he wasn't,' Steiner commented softly as the blue convoy tail-light of the last tank began to disappear in the snowy grey gloom of the new dawn. Suddenly he wished that the unknown *Ami* paras could give the supremely confident Panzer General a nasty bloody nose whenever the two forces bumped into each other as they undoubtedly would this 20th December. Then he dismissed the thought as unworthy of a German soldier. 'All right, Todt, take that look off yer nasty mug and let's get on our way.'

'Where to, sir?'

'To the River Sure. Whatever Lieutenant-General Fritz Bayerlein thinks to the contrary, I know that his panzer boys are going to be needing the Paras one of these days soon.' Todt reacted with alacrity. He swung round and bellowed at the top of his voice, as if he were back on the parade ground at Stendhal, 'All right, you bunch of miserable-looking wet tails, let's be having you ... *march*!'

A moment later the sorry collection of frozen, injured paras disappeared into the grey whirling dawn, bound — unknowingly — on their collision course with T-Force.

CHAPTER 3

The advance guard of the Panzer Lehr rolled into Mageret at seven o'clock. The light of the new day crept in behind them feebly, as if reluctant to illuminate a crazy world, torn by war. There was a sudden crackle of small arms fire. A boxlike American ambulance, its big red cross riddled with bullet holes, shot abruptly out of a side street and crashed into the wall ahead of Bayerlein's half-track. The driver, his neck broken, slumped unconscious over the wheel. From the ruptured doors, the screaming, bandaged wounded attempted to creep away over the snow. They didn't get far!

A frightened Belgian civilian was thrust in front of the impatient tank commander. In fluent French, Bayerlein asked: 'Have you seen any other Americans?'

'A lot of them, *mon General*,' the shabby runt of a civilian quavered, eager to help. 'A great force went through here a few hours ago.' He pointed a finger which trembled east down the main highway to Longvilly. 'At least fifty tanks and forty armoured cars. And they were led ... by ... by a General.'

Bayerlein dismissed the shivering civilian with an angry wave. Now he could make out the sound of tank motors to the east. The civilian shuffled away, head bent to hide the light in his eyes. When he was out of sight of the Germans he spat in the snow. '*Sales Boches!*' he cursed under his breath. The Americans he had seen had been panic-stricken refugees from the crumbling front heading for the safety of Luxembourg.

But a suddenly worried General Bayerlein did not know that. Some of his confidence of the early morning began to drain from him. Was there American armour out there somewhere on his flank after all, just waiting for him to drive forward to Bastogne before it smacked him in the flank — hard? Abruptly he made a decision — the wrong one.

'All right,' he ordered, 'we move towards Neffe, *but carefully*! There could well be *Ami* armour up there, waiting for us.' Cautiously, very cautiously, with a heavy tank now positioned in front of his half-track, Bayerlein led his men up the Longvilly-Bastogne highway. It took him nearly an hour to cover two kilometres. Just before the village of Neffe, the column ran into a minefield. The lead Panther came to a sudden halt, its right track flapping out in front of it in the abruptly black-scorched snow like a broken limb.

'*Grosse Kacke am Christbaum!*' Bayerlein cursed angrily, as the Panther's crew, their black uniforms already smouldering, bailed out hurriedly and threw themselves into the snow. 'What damn next?' He cupped his hands around his mouth and bellowed, 'Get those asparagus Tarzans of engineers up here and let's have these mines cleared — *at the double!*'

His Chief of Staff watched Bayerlein curiously. It was unlike the Divisional Commander to be flustered by a few mines. Normally he would have just ordered up another tank to chance its luck and clear a path for the column one way or the other. The Chief was losing his usual fiery dash. He shook his head in annoyance and told himself that it would be mid-morning before the Wehrmacht's élite panzer division reached Neffe if Bayerlein continued to proceed in this highly untypical, cautious manner.

Four miles west of the stalled German column, a long column of unwashed, unshaven infantry was plodding down the snowy highway towards Neffe, too. Many were without helmets, most of them minus overcoats — there were even a few without weapons. But their step was quick, and bold and jaunty, as they advanced through the grey gloom to an unknown destination to fight an unknown foe. For on their shoulder they wore the white and black shoulder patch of the Screaming Eagle. The 101st Airborne had arrived at the front, and after being dragged so surprisingly from their soft billets just outside Paris, the mecca of all GIs, and driven in freezing open trucks right across France, they were ready to fight anybody and everybody.

Stragglers from Mageret began to pass, their eyes downcast as if ashamed of themselves. A bare-headed Para armed with bazooka made way for a great towed 155mm cannon to pass and jeered at the weary Lieutenant sitting frozen-faced next to the driver, 'Hey, lieutenant, what about trading your shooting iron for this here little old bean shooter?' 'Yeah,' someone else added, 'and why don't ya stick around and show us how to fire the goddam thing?'

The cannon was followed by a bunch of red-eyed, gaunt infantry, who had long thrown away their weapons. 'Where in hell are you guys going?' one of them asked.

A para, armed only with a stick, waved it threateningly to the east. 'To fight Krauts, of course!' he cried.

The straggler looked at the para cynically. 'We've had it,' he grunted sullenly, 'and you're gonna get it!' He slouched on after his foot-sore, beaten companions.

'Just take a goddam look at those Geronimos!' poker-faced Colonel Ewell, their commander, said in undisguised admiration to his artillery commander, Colonel Sherburne, as his 501st Parachute Regiment filed by. 'You'd think they were off on a goddam picnic, wouldn't you?'

'You sure would, Julian!' Sherburne replied, equally enthusiastically. 'When it comes down to cases, the

Geronimos—' He stopped short. Ahead in the fog, there was the sudden, high-pitched hysterical burst of a German machinegun. '*Spandau*!' he identified it immediately. 'The point has bumped into the Heinies!'

Ewell, veteran of Normandy and Holland, reacted at once. 'You ain't kidding, brother!' He swung round to his battalion commanders, standing at the roadside next to him. 'Okay, fellers, let's get on the ball. Get the two lead companies on either side of the road… Send word to the 2nd Battalion, I want them to take the village of Bizory — it's somewhere up there on the left…' Order followed order in rapid succession. Then Ewell's hard face cracked into a semblance of a smile, a rare thing with him. 'Clear up the situation,' he concluded in his normal tone. 'But listen gentlemen, I don't want you to beat the enemy to death!'

Laughing uproariously, his officers doubled away to their waiting men to carry out the Colonel's orders.

Momentarily turning his back on Bastogne, Bayerlein conducting his operations from a cave not far from Neffe Station, turned his attention to Longvilly. First he would wipe out the threat to his flank from Longvilly; then he would take Bastogne.

At two o'clock that afternoon he launched his attack on the little town. The halted column of stragglers in their vehicles stretching from Longvilly to Mageret offered a tempting target. The whole weight of Bayerlein's artillery descended upon it. With a tremendous elemental roar, the eighty-eights streamed from the grey sky. The stragglers did not wait for the second salvo. Screaming with fear, they scrambled from the burning, wrecked vehicles, leaving their wounded lying behind on the road and broke across the fields, throwing their weapons away as they ran.

Bayerlein's Panthers hurried forward, grinding over the dead and dying, their tracks a sudden bright red. They clattered across the road, littered with the burning mess of wrecked, abandoned jeeps, Shermans, armoured cars, self-propelled guns, and started into the fields, to disappear into the fog of war.

But they didn't get far. The paras of the 101st were waiting for them on the snowy heights. The first scarlet flash of a bazooka cut the grey gloom frighteningly. A tank reeled backwards on its rear sprockets, as if it had suddenly run into a thick brick wall. In an instant it was burning, its tracer ammunition zig-zagging crazily into the sky. The first bazooka round seemed to act as a signal. Abruptly the whole front erupted with violent fire. Another of Bayerlein's tanks was hit and came to an abrupt halt in the snow, a gleaming silver hole in its side, greedy little flames already shooting out from below its engine-cowling. And another! The follow-up infantry hesitated. The ragged skirmish line wavered. Angrily the German officers blew their whistles. Red-faced NCOs bellowed at the hesitant men and forced them forward with blows from their rifle-butts and heavy boots. They started to advance again. Heavily they lumbered through the snowy fields, crying hoarsely, their grey coat-tails flapping around their boots.

It was the target Ewell's angry, frozen paras had been waiting for ever since they had been alerted for action and forced out of their cushy billets in France the day before. All their pent-up fury at the cold, the war, the enemy went into that first mighty volley of small arms fire. It stopped the German infantry dead. Like a wave being broken by a hidden reef, the enemy attack came to a halt. Suddenly there were dead and dying Germans lying everywhere on the snow-covered base of the hill-line.

But they came again — and again! Three times they were rallied by their officers and forced into that murderous fire, their numbers getting ever fewer. They died by the score in the fields below, trapped by the Belgian wire fences which were everywhere, hit time and time again by the American slugs so that in the end the bodies hanging on the wire looked like bundles of blood-stained rags.

Finally as the snow started to swirl down, increasing its fury at every moment, as if some God on high was determined to blot out the monstrous scene of death and destruction below, they gave up. Their attack petered out. Under the cover of the snow, the German survivors began to fall back on Neffe, dragging their bloody wounded with them, while above them on the heights the exhausted Geronimos collapsed over their smoking weapons. Now the Longvilly road was free for the follow-up battalions of 101st Airborne to begin their march into Bastogne. The Americans had won the race for the key road centre and in his dripping, icy post in the cave, a frustrated, angry *Generalleutnant* Bayerlein knew that the siege of Bastogne had begun…

CHAPTER 4

T-Force had now left Ettelbruck behind. The few scared civilians, who had been on the streets as they had rattled through the little Luxembourg town, had turned their faces away as they had done so, as if they had not wanted even to see the Americans. And when van Fleet had attempted to ask for directions from one of the civilians in French, the man had mumbled something in the incomprehensible Luxembourg dialect and disappeared down a side-alley swiftly, as if the devil himself were after him. 'Bugger him,' a frozen Limey had commented mournfully, 'with sods like that for allies, we don't need no enemies, do we, sir?' Hardt had not replied; his eyes had been fixed anxiously on the snowy hills ahead.

Now they were rumbling cautiously through the vast empty white landscape like a little trail of insignificant black ants. The going was murderous. Each new climb was an all-out fight with the elements. Time and time again one of the T-Force armoured vehicles would begin to slip in the deep snow. Desperately its sweating, cursing driver would fight the controls, trying to prevent it from careening into one of the deep drainage ditches which bounded the road north on both sides. Sometimes Old Baldy, which was at the point, would teeter on the very edge of the ditch, see-sawing back and forth, its engine roaring impotently, with Wheels, the ex-New York cabbie, using all his skill to keep the half-track from plunging over. As Dutchie, a devout Catholic, commented more than once, 'Goddamit, Wheels, the Big Man up there in the clouds must like you!'

Once one of the Staghound armoured cars slid off the road and crashed into the ditch. The whole column came to a halt. While the sentries doubled out on both sides and took up their positions in the snow under Big Red's command, the rest of T-Force began the back-breaking job of freeing the stricken vehicle. With fingers that felt like enormous swollen sausages, the shivering GIs attached a steel hawser to the back of Old Baldy. Twice it parted like a piece of wet cotton under the strain. But finally, Wheels managed to get the Staghound back on the road and the exhausted, frozen men could crawl back to their own vehicles.

Now the wind seemed to be coming straight from Siberia. Sweeping in from the east across the hills, it spread an icy layer of freezing snow over the T-Force cannon, metal decks, bodies. Some of the GIs wept with the sheer pain of it all. Icicles hung from the stubble of their unshaven chins. The dewdrops froze at the end of their scarlet noses. Every time they opened their mouths beneath their scarves to breathe out, the air stabbed them to the very lungs. To touch metal was like grasping a red-hot poker, which ripped the flesh off uncovered fingers cruelly.

'Christ, skipper,' van Fleet gasped, his helmet white with snow, his frozen cheeks ashen. 'We can't keep this up much longer ... the guys are —'

'I know, Clarry,' Hardt cut him short, his breath clouding the freezing air in a thick grey fog. 'Do you think I'm made of goddam stone! But we've got to get across the Sure before the Krauts get there? Angrily he nodded to the east. Barely visible through the white wall of streaming snow, van Fleet could just make out a faint pink glow. 'You know what that is, don't you?' Van Fleet nodded. It was Kraut artillery fire and it couldn't be more than a couple of miles away.

Grimly the armoured column plunged on through the howling, snow-heavy countryside.

Time passed leadenly. Here and there a young T-Force man closed his eyes, the tears frozen to his cheeks like cold pearls, and prayed fervently for death. But still Hardt did not relent. Blinded by the flying snow, face purple with the icy wind, he stood up in the front of the clattering half-track next to a cursing Wheels, searching the white fields ahead for the first sign of the little river. Twice Big Red offered to take his place as lookout and twice the Major refused with a curt, 'Leave it to me, Red ... I know what I'm doing!'

And then when it seemed the cruel snow would never stop, the flying flakes grew fewer and fewer, finally ceasing altogether. 'Sodding hell,' Limey crouched behind Hardt, breathed, 'will wonders never cease, sir... Look over there!' He pointed a trembling finger to the east. Slowly, as if his head were worked by stiff springs, Hardt followed the direction of his gaze.

A pale December sun was attempting to break through the grey gloom above them. But it wasn't the sun which attracted his attention. It was a small cluster of dirty-white houses, grouped around a little church with a pointed steeple, to the right of the road, the grey snake of fast-running water beyond in the valley.

'Bourscheid, if I'm not mistaken,' Hardt croaked in sudden triumph, 'and brother if that isn't the River Sure, I'll eat my helmet, liner as well...'

'It looks OK, Major,' Big Red gasped and wiped his scummed, frost-cracked lips with the back of his big hand. 'Me and Triggerman went right through the village. Not a living soul.' He gestured to the east and the ever-increasing noise of the

German guns, 'I guess the civvies bugged out because of that.'

'Trust a goddam civvie to do that,' Triggerman snarled, his dark, olive-skinned face as sour as ever. 'It's the same the world over. We GIs do all the dirty work and them chickenshit civvies —'

Major Hardt held up his hand. 'Okay, Triggerman, spare me the lecture on the iniquities of the civilian world,' he commanded, a faint smile on his face. The undersized ex-Mafia man seemed to hate everything and everybody, except T-Force. 'We've got a lot to do before dark.' He turned to Big Red again. 'What about the River?'

'Well, we didn't go right down to it, as you ordered, Major. But we got a pretty good gander at it from the church-tower. Couldn't see a thing and I checked for footprints in the snow with glasses like you told me to.' Big Red shook his head. 'Nix. Nary a sign of a Kraut nor nobody else for that matter, sir.'

'What about you, Clarry?'

Lieutenant van Fleet slapped the rest of the snow from his trousers, still elegantly creased in spite of the fact he had been crouching in a bush overlooking the valley for the last thirty minutes, his glasses focused on the little stone bridge below. 'Not a movement anywhere. As Red here says — nary a sign of a Kraut.'

Hardt tugged the end of his red pinched nose and considered. It looked almost too good to be true. The enemy was only a matter of a couple of miles away. They knew this countryside like the back of their hand; after all they had occupied it for four years. Why then had they neglected to send out a recon patrol to capture the vital bridge, which could bar any advance on the Ettelbruck road to hit the flank of their armoured advance on Bastogne? Yet such oversights were always happening in war. A bridge, a crossroads, an outhouse, which at the outset of a battle could have been taken for a handful of men, would be overlooked and cost the lives of hundreds of soldiers later. He made up his mind. 'All right, Clarry — Red — this is what we're gonna do. I'm gonna put our muscle up front on the road — the two Staghounds. They'll rush the bridge. OK?'

The two men nodded their heads in silence. All around the T-Force men had stopped spooning the frozen hash out of the little olive-drab cans and were listening attentively to their commander's instructions.

'But just to make sure, I'm gonna put a platoon of infantry in on the left of the bridge. You'll lead it, Red, assembling near that copse of firs.'

'Sir!'

'Clarry, you'll take another platoon and cross the river just beyond that barn or outhouse or whatever it is.'

'Roger, sir.' Instinctively the Lieutenant's hand fell to his knife, tucked into the side of his combat boot. If there were Krauts up there on the far bank of the little river, the deadly knife would be the weapon he would use on them.

'I'll follow up the armoured cars with the half-track and rush the heights beyond, once they're across. The rest of you will follow — at the double!'

Major Hardt looked around the faces of his men. They were alert again and ready to go. He knew he could rely upon them. 'Okay, fellers,' he commanded, 'let's get on the stick!... *Roll 'em!*'

As always, Red felt himself bound to echo any order given by Major Hardt, as if the men were not capable of understanding the original without his help. 'Okay, youse guys,' he bellowed. 'You heard what the CO said. Get the lead out ya butts — and let's go!'

'Here the *Amis* come, lads!' the Para Corporal whispered, as if the men advancing cautiously across the snowfield might hear him. 'Get ready!'

Camouflaged expertly in the clump of snow-heavy firs which lined the other bank of the Sure, just above the little stone bridge, they tensed over their automatic weapons. The man armed with the survivors' only *Panzerfaust* crouched behind the wall, ready to meet the advancing armoured cars, while down by the water, the engineer readied his fuse.

The Corporal looked around, pleased. The landing from the first Junkers had been one big mess. Half the platoon had been blown away by the high wind and although they had searched most of the night for Major Steiner, they had been unsuccessful. Still, the Corporal, a veteran of Cassino and Normandy, was used to acting on his own. It was part of the paratrooper's creed — if in doubt, *act!*' Now Major Steiner or no Major Steiner, he knew it was his duty to stop the little band of *Amis* from crossing the bridge.

With professional interest, the Corporal watched the *Amis* approach. Obviously the two slow-moving, six-wheeled armoured cars were bait. If there were any enemy troops on the other side of the ravine, the *Ami* commander probably reasoned, they would concentrate on the armoured cars. In the meantime he would slip his two platoons of infantry across the water. The Corporal grinned to himself, but his dark eyes remained hard. Well, he told himself, the *Ami* commander was in for a nasty surprise. The Sure, to one hundred metres on both sides of the bridge, was at least three metres deep and if that didn't stop the Amis, it was running at six kilometres an hour. Without boats, the *Amis* simply couldn't get across. Slowly the Corporal started to raise his sniper's rifle and line it up on the head of the leading armoured car commander. The

Amis were not going to cross the Sure this particular grey December afternoon. With a little sigh of satisfaction, as if he were descending upon the beautifully nubile body of his current mistress back in his native Berlin, he fitted the rifle butt more snugly into his shoulder. The *Amis* grew closer and closer.

In low gear the first Staghound rolled ever closer to the silent bridge. Inside the green glowing turret, the radio chattered incessantly, as the operator kept in touch with the second armoured car two hundred yards behind. If the first one were hit, the second car was to take over; it was standard operating procedure. But the commander left that to his radio operator; his attention was concentrated fully and totally on the stone bridge. He had ridden point for T-Force ever since Normandy now and somehow he had an uneasy feeling that his luck was beginning to run out. Only a couple of days ago he had lost his rabbit foot, and in Ettelbruck a black cat had run straight in front of his Staghound — it had narrowly escaped being crushed under the armoured car's six wheels. Angrily the commander dismissed his forebodings; they were just a lot of goddam nonsense. Taking a grip of himself, he straightened up his upper body, as if to display to the watching world just how little he cared for such superstition. There was a single light crack like that of a dry twig being snapped underfoot in a hot summer. The car commander's mouth dropped open stupidly, his eyes full of sudden disbelief that this terrible thing was happening to him. Slowly but inevitably he began to slump down into the turret.

'*Hiram!*' the radio operator began.

His words were drowned by the crash of the *Panzerfaust*. A dark object wobbled awkwardly through the air, trailing angry fiery sparks behind it. There was the hollow boom of metal striking metal. The whole turret glowed a frightening dull red. Next instant the armoured car had come to a stop, burning fiercely.

Up on the height above, a thrill of fear ran through Hardt and an awful groan came from deep down inside him. 'Christ on a crutch!' he cried, 'we walked into a goddam trap!'

'*Now!*' Big Red yelled in fury. He lobbed the grenade across the river and as it exploded with an angry red crump on the far bank, doubled forward. Behind him the T-Force ran towards the water, spraying the bushes on the other side from the hip as they advanced.

A German in a green camouflage suit jumped up from a pit. Triggerman fired a quick burst. The German's hands fanned the air frantically, as he fell back in his hole, gurgling sickeningly from a shattered windpipe. Another German tried to lob a stick grenade at them. Dutchie Schulze tore his face away with a vicious salvo. He slumped forward, his face looking as if someone had thrown a handful of strawberry jam at it. The potato masher exploded harmlessly in mid-stream, throwing up a huge spout of boiling, angry white water.

Big Red hit the water. Enemy fire was hissing across it angrily everywhere now. Some of the T-Force hesitated. 'Come on, you chicken-shit bastards!' he roared in fury at the sudden trap which had been sprung upon them, 'today you earn your goddam pay!' Without a second look behind him, he waded into it. Realising that standing on the snowy bank, they would be sitting ducks for the Germans hidden in the bushes above, the rest of T-Force followed.

Almost instantly, they could feel the icy tug of the boiling water at their feet. Red, his face set with angry determination, continued wading forward, firing from the hip as he went. The icy water reached to his knees. He could hardly withstand the force. Just behind him a trooper screamed with pain. '*I'm hit —*' Before he could finish his cry, he had slipped on the smooth pebbles under his feet. Desperately Red grabbed for him. He missed. In an instant the wounded man was floating down the stream, fighting frantically to regain his feet, trailing a stream of blood behind, '*Save*' — the last cry died on his lips, as the boiling water submerged him.

Another man was hit. And another. The cruel current snatched them with greedy fingers. Screaming for help, they were swept away before their comrades could help them. For a moment more, Big Red fought his way forward. But the water was too tough for even his gigantic body. Supporting the platoon's radio operator, who had been hit in the shoulder, and preventing him from going under, he swung round and cried fervently. '*Back … get back… Let's get the goddam hell outa here!*'

The survivors needed no urging. Gasping frantically with the effort, bullets hissing over the surface of the water everywhere, they began to struggle back the way they had come. Now it was up to the remaining Staghound.

The six-wheeled armoured car sped recklessly over the snow-covered road, its six-pounder pumping shot after shot at the far bank, its machinegun spraying the bushes just beyond the bridge with tracer. Now it had negotiated the burning lead car and was only a matter of yards away from the vital bridge. Hardt lowered his glasses for a moment. 'All right, you mortarmen, don't stand around there like a collection of spare pricks — give him goddam covering fire!'

The loader acted at once. He dropped the bomb into the tube and swung back, his fingers thrust into his ears. The gunner fired. There was a soft obscene plop. Hardt flashed a quick look upwards and caught a glimpse of the plump mortar bomb sailing through the air towards the opposite bank. Good, he told himself, that will keep the Krauts' head down. A moment later it exploded beyond the bridge, sending a stream of brown earth mingled with the white of the snow high into the air.

Swiftly Hardt took up his glasses again. Behind him the mortarmen started to warm up to their work. Bomb after bomb hurtled through the air. The tight valley echoed and re-echoed furiously to the thunder of war. Hardt focused on the Staghound. It was nearly up to the bridge now. Hardt tensed. He had nearly done it! A minute more and he'd be across. The armoured car's front wheels bumped over the ramp. Hardt caught his breath. The car was in the centre of the bridge now. The gunner had ceased firing, as if he already had realised he had pulled it off; he had gotten T-Force across the Sure. Grinning with sudden happiness, Major Hardt swung round, 'Okay, you mortarmen —'

Hardt's command was drowned by a sudden thick crump, which grew and grew in volume by the instant. Below the little bridge trembled wildly like a live thing. Great chunks of stone began to drop into the water below. A horrified Hardt saw the deep crack which was starting to run across the bridge's centre. Desperately the Staghound's driver pushed his foot down on the gas pedal. He *had* to get across before the bridge disintegrated! To no avail! Hardt dug his nails cruelly into the palms of his hands, his body lathered in a sudden sweat, and willed him across. But that wasn't to be. Abruptly the Staghound started to tremble with ever increasing violence as the bridge swayed and began falling apart. The six-wheeled car, teetered on the edge of the crack, swung back and forth like a toy. '*No!*' Hardt cried out loud. '*No* ...'

With a great resounding crash the bridge broke. The armoured car shot through the air. Like a stone it disappeared into the suddenly white boiling water below; and as it did, Major Hardt knew with the abrupt clarity of a vision that T-Force's first attempt to find a way across the River Sure had failed lamentably.

PART THREE: ON THE ROAD

'Tomorrow morning … Bastogne will fall into your hands like an overripe plum.'

General Baron von Manteuffel to his commanders, December 22nd, 1944.

CHAPTER 1

In spite of the freezing cold and the snow which was drifting down as if it would never stop, General Patton remained rigidly at the position of attention, while the last of the Fourth Armoured Shermans clattered by, heading north. His favourite armoured division had had a rough trip these last two days from the Saar front to the new one in Luxembourg; yet that alone did not account for the tankers' weariness and the state of their mud encrusted Shermans. The Division, which had been at the point of his advance ever since Normandy, was worn out, he knew. It had had too many casualties and most of its tanks were the original ones with which the Division had first come to the European theatre of operations. Most of them had long been ripe for the scrapheap. Still, Patton told himself, as the final Sherman ground by the *Gare* and began to rattle in low gear up the incline which led out of the city, the Fourth was the only armoured division he had available for the drive to Bastogne.

With a sigh of relief he dropped his saluting arm and relaxed his 'war face', as he called the fierce, aggressive look he always gave his troops when they were going into battle. Stiffly he stepped from the jeep, from which he had been conducting the great turnabout these last forty-eight hours and said to his sergeant driver, 'Okay Mims, park her beneath the Alpha and go and get yourself some hot chow. I won't need you any more this day — thank God!'

The driver grinned and tried to cheer his weary boss up. 'General, the government is wasting a lot of dough, hiring a whole general staff. Hell, you and me has run the Third Army all day and done a better job than they do!'

Patton smiled thinly, but his faded blue eyes did not light up; he was too tired. 'I guess you might be right at that, Mims. G'night!'

'G'night, General.'

Feeling all of his sixty years, the tall, lean Commander of the Third Army made his way to the Alpha's swing door. He pushed aside the thick felt blackout curtain a little irritably. The assembled staff officers sprang to attention. They knew Patton's fiery reaction to any breach of military courtesy. But this evening the General did not seem to notice them; he was too weary and too preoccupied with his coming offensive. He passed through their suddenly silent ranks, as if they weren't there, ignored the PFC holding open the iron gate of the elevator, and began to ascend the stairs, stamping the snow from his gleaming riding boots as he did so.

The senior officer of the 4th Armoured were waiting for him on the second floor — one-eyed General Gaffey, who had once been his own Chief of Staff, and Dager and Abrams, the heads of the Fourth's main Combat Commands. Hastily they put down their sandwiches as Patton entered, and snapped to attention. Patton waved for them to relax. 'Keep eating, gentlemen,' he ordered and walked slowly to the big map, 'God knows where you might get your next meal.'

Gaffey, who had just taken over the Fourth, laughed a little uncertainly, not knowing whether to take Patton's remark as a joke or not. But the two veteran tank commanders knew differently. Greedily they bit into the spam sandwiches, as if they might be the last they would ever eat.

'Okay gentlemen, I'll give it to you straight,' Patton commenced his briefing. 'It's gonna be tough, real tough. I'm giving the Fourth the honour of relieving those stupid bastards of paratroopers who have gone and gotten their goddam selves surrounded in Bastogne!'

Abrams paused in the middle of a bite, his chubby face covered in a weary grin. 'Don't you think, sir, you could kinda give that sort of honour to somebody else for a change? The Fourth has been *honoured* a helluva lot these last five months.'

For the first time that long December day, Patton smiled. 'Creighton,' he said to his favourite combat commander, 'there just ain't anybody else — so you're stuck with it. Okay, this is the way you're going to do it.' Swiftly and expertly, Patton explained that the drive for Bastogne would kick off with armour in the lead. The main body of the armoured infantry would be kept in reserve. Whenever the Fourth encountered stiff resistance, the infantry should be brought up to envelope the German strongpoints. Every care should be taken not to let the drive get bogged down in an infantry battle.

'General,' Gaffey reacted first, a little angry that the Army Commander was dictating his tactics to him — after all that was the job of a divisional commander. 'I agree with what you say. But that corridor we're gonna bulldoze to Bastogne is kind of self-sealing, if you follow me? You see, once the armour's through, the Krauts can cut it behind us at any time. And besides that, if we're not supposed to get bogged down in an all-out infantry battle, what happens if the Krauts plant a real humdinger of a strongpoint to our front?' He licked his suddenly dry lips and fell silent, wondering if he had said too much. He knew Patton's explosive temper of old.

But Patton remained calm. 'I read you, Hugh,' he answered slowly. 'I read you well. Okay, I'm gonna get Air to cover your rear. As soon as the Krauts start to concentrate anywhere along your flanks, the fly-boys will hit them.'

'In this weather, sir!' Dager protested, speaking for the first time. 'They tell me TAC AIR has been socked in since the start of the Kraut offensive.'

'Yes, yes,' Patton agreed impatiently. 'But I'm gonna deal with it.'

Gaffey wondered how exactly Patton was going to 'deal' with the weather, but he didn't press the point; he had to protect Dager. 'And the strongpoint, sir?' he urged.

'I've got T-Force up there somewhere in Luxembourg, scouting for you. Whenever you hit trouble, they'll find a fresh route for you,' Patton said with more confidence than he felt. It was now over eighteen hours since he had last heard from Hardt. 'You can rely on them.'

Abrams, his mouth full of spam and dark Luxembourg bread nodded his head in agreement. He had worked with T-Force in France; he knew its reputation. 'Sure, General, if anybody can bull us a way through, it'll be the tough tittie outfit.'

There was a low ripple of laughter from the others. Patton grinned. The tension vanished. 'Okay, gentlemen, finish your chow, then get to your commands.' His smile vanished. 'Hugh, kick off your attack at zero six hundred hours tomorrow.'

The Fourth's commanders clicked to attention. Patton raised his right hand to his thinning silver hair to acknowledge the salute. 'Now gentlemen, I'm off to see God — *about the goddam weather!*'

And with that he passed out of the room, leaving them to stare at his back in open-mouthed amazement...

Chaplain O'Neil, the Third Army's Chaplain, looked at Patton like a rabbit which had just been cornered by a fox. It wasn't often he was called into the General's presence. But when he was, it always meant trouble: get God working on the Third

Army's VD rate, which was keeping too many riflemen out of the line; a special prayer to prevent trench feet among the infantry; did the Church have some special power to ensure that the Third Army got more gasoline than the 1st and 9th Armies? General Patton really seemed to believe that the Almighty was working for him and the Third Army!

Now he waited in fearful anticipation for Patton's command. The Third Army Commander took his time. He puffed contentedly at his long Havana, examined its mouthpiece, as if there were something of considerable importance hidden there, placed it in his mouth again, blew a slow smoke ring to the ceiling and finally said: 'Chaplain, I don't believe much in those folk who talk a lot about the weather and do goddam nothing about it — excuse my French, Chaplain,' he added hastily.

O'Neil nodded his forgiveness warily, wondering what was coming next; he had experienced Patton's buildups to the subject under discussion before.

'Now Chaplain,' Patton continued, pointing his cigar at the nervous priest, as if he intended to assault him with it, 'I'm sick and tired of my soldiers having to fight mud and floods as well as Germans. I want you to pray for dry weather. See if you can't get God to work on our side.'

Chaplain O'Neil goggled at the General incredulously. For a moment he was too surprised to speak, then he stuttered: 'Sir … it's going to take pretty thick rug for that kind of praying.'

'I don't care if it takes a flying carpet,' Patton replied, 'I want you to get up a prayer for good weather.'

'Yessir,' O'Neill said. 'But permit me to say, General, that it isn't the customary thing among men of my profession to pray for good weather to kill our fellow men.'

Patton's thin face flushed. 'Chaplain,' he rasped in his high-pitched voice, 'are you teaching me theology or are you the

Chaplain of the Third Army? I want a prayer — and quick. Goddamit, I'm starting a new push tomorrow morning at six!'

'Yessir … at once, sir.'

Hurriedly Chaplain O'Neill backed out of the room. Outside he bumped into Colonel Harkins and swiftly told him what happened during the interview with the General. 'What do you think the Old Man wants, Harkins?' he asked finally. The Colonel grinned at the Chaplain's red-faced confusion. 'I can tell you what the Old Man wants, Chaplain. He wants a prayer and he wants it right now because he'll publish it then to the Command as soon as the attack starts. Psychology, you see?'

But Chaplain O'Neill did not see. Shaking his head and muttering to himself that this was 'a real tough baby', he wandered off to his room to begin composing the General's special prayer.

Alone in his big room, watching the blue circles of smoke ascend slowly to the dirty ceiling, feeling abruptly exhausted, deflated, all confidence drained out of his long, lean body. Patton stared into nothing.

Outside the Fourth's deuce-and-a-half trucks were still continuing to move to the new front in a steady stream and from the direction of the station there came the rusty chatter of shunting locomotives. Their noise drowned the rumble of the German guns; but instinctively the suddenly reflective General knew they were there: a tangible reminder of how precarious his position here in Luxembourg was. In exactly twelve hours, his favourite division — the Fourth — would be plunging into the unknown, its equipment worn out, its men weary veterans or green replacements, advancing through the coldest winter Europe had known since 1910.

Would Gaffey be able to pull it off under such conditions, fighting as he was in the dark? Angrily Patton stubbed out his big cigar on the edge of his chair, not noticing the sudden stink of charred wood. '*Goddamit*,' he cried out aloud to no one in particular, '*where in all hell's name is T-Force?*'

CHAPTER 2

If General Patton had known at that moment what was happening in a lonely Belgian farmhouse only a score of miles away from his Luxembourg HQ, he would have had even more reason for his sudden gloom. For as night started to fall over the battlefield and the rumble of the guns began to die away, General Baron Hasso von Manteuffel was already planning his own all-out attack on Bastogne.

That afternoon he had learnt to his anger that the point of Bayerlein's Panzer Lehr had been stopped by a hastily erected American road barrier. Immediately von Manteuffel had motored out to the road block himself. The young sullen Lieutenant in charge of the point had been arrested and relieved of his command; later he would be court-martialled for cowardice. Furious at such hesitation, Manteuffel had clambered up onto the turret of the first tank himself and had taken charge himself. 'Go round the roadblock,' he had bellowed at the driver. 'Head for St Hubert, I tell you we have a clear road!'

And Manteuffel had been proven right. For an hour the five tank patrol, led personally by the undersized, cocky Army Commander had swept through supposedly 'heavily defended enemy territory' with impunity. Not a shot had been fired at them and they had not seen one single *Ami*.

Now the little General faced his two armoured division commanders, Bayerlein and gross, monocled von Luettwitz, commander of the 2nd Panzer, and delivered his orders for the morrow. They were simple, direct and brutal. 'Gentlemen, both the 2nd Panzer and the Panzer Lehr will continue their drive for the Meuse. That is objective number one. Objective number two is Bastogne!' He looked at the faces of his two subordinates in the flickering unreal light of the guttering candle, the barn HQ's only light. 'My experiences this afternoon tell me you are taking the American opposition too seriously.'

'But General,' von Luettwitz, who was also the Panzer corps commander, protested, 'we haven't got sufficient infantry for an all-out attack on Bastogne!'

'You don't need it. All you need is determination and courage. You will blast your way forward from the west with artillery. Bring the damn place down about the *Amis'* heads with your guns and then go in with your tanks.' Von Manteuffel thrust his small, delicate-looking hand into the wavering light, his fingers outstretched. 'Tomorrow morning, *meine Herren*, Bastogne will fall into your hands like an over-ripe plum and believe me, you will crush —' it his jaw hardened aggressively, as he pressed his fingers together with brutal suddenness, *'just like that...'**

A thick white mantle of fog covered the sombre, shell-shattered buildings of the 10lst's HQ at Bastogne that morning. It gave the besieged town an air of peace and security. The staff officers had breakfasted on hot pancakes and syrup, three to each officer, dispensed by the grinning Chinese cook Chuck Wong. But that and the apparent calm was not the only reason for the Airborne men's relaxed, confident mood that Friday morning. Just after breakfast they had received two messages from Patton's HQ which had given the beleaguered men new hope. One had read: 'Re-supply by air will start coming at twenty hundred hours'. The other: 'Hugh is coming!' And it hadn't taken General McAuliffe, the 101st Commander, long to figure out who 'Hugh' was.

'It's Hugh Gaffey,' he had explained to his puzzled staff. *'Gaffey of the Fourth Armoured!'* His broad face had broken out in a relieved grin. 'And fellers if the Fourth is on its way to relieve us, I guess I can afford a little sack-time.'

Now, while the General slept for the first time in forty-eight hours, the 101st's suddenly confident officers kept cocking their ears to one side or gazing southwards out of the HQ's shattered windows, waiting for the rattle of tank tracks which would indicate the arrival of Patton's favourite division. But the first troops to arrive at Bastogne's southern outskirts that day were fated not to be American; they were Germans!

Three miles south of Bastogne, Sergeant Oswald Butler, in charge of a roadblock on the highway to Arlon, suddenly spotted them, advancing boldly up the road, carrying what looked like a bedsheet attached to a pole — four of them in drab field-grey. Hastily he whirled the handle of his field telephone and called his commanding officer, 'Captain,' he exclaimed, 'there're four Krauts coming up the road. They're carrying a white flag. Looks as if they want to surrender.'

'Okay, Butler,' his CO replied easily, 'go out and bring 'em in.'

But the four Germans did not want to surrender. They wanted to put General von Leuttwitz's proposal to the Americans. 'We are parlementaires,' they explained in careful English, 'we want to talk to your commanding officer.'

Butler hesitated; then he made a decision. 'Okay, but I've gotta blindfold you. I don't want you guys spying on our positions.'

He reached up and began to tear strips off the dirty white flag; then stepped forward to the first German officer. Tamely he allowed himself to be blindfolded. Later, he reasoned, once Bastogne was German, he could reckon up with the insolent, uncouth American. Moments later, the strange, hesitant little procession of Americans and Germans began to make its way back to the 101st lines.

The Colonel handed a tousled-haired, yawning General McAuliffe the German message, but the General shoved it back at him. 'You read it,' he said thickly.

The Colonel did so: 'There is only one possibility to save the encircled USA troops from total annihilation: that is the honourable surrender of the encircled town.' He hesitated.

'Get on with it, man,' McAuliffe growled.

'If this proposal should be rejected, one German Artillery Corps and six heavy AA Battalions are ready to annihilate the USA troops in and near Bastogne... All the serious civilian losses caused by this artillery fire would not correspond with the well-known American humanity,' the Colonel's voice died away and he looked at his sleepy Divisional Commander expectantly.

McAuliffe ran his hands through his dark hair. '*Oh shit!*' he cursed in disgust. Seizing his helmet, he swept by the Colonel to grab some fresh air.

When he returned, the Colonel told him the Germans were still waiting for a formal answer. They had presented a written ultimatum; they expected a written answer.

McAuliffe nodded his understanding. 'But what in hell's name should I tell them?' he asked angrily, toying with his pencil. 'How about that first remark of yours, General?' someone suggested.

'Hell no!' McAuliffe answered with a smile. 'I'll leave that kind of language to old Blood and Guts Patton. But what about something similar?'

'What, General?' the assembled staff officers cried.

'This!' McAuliffe answered and seizing his pencil wrote hastily on a scrap of paper. 'Here,' he handed the message to the Colonel who had awakened him. 'You read it to them.'

The Colonel read:

'To the German Commander:
NUTS!
The American Commander.'

The tight conference room exploded with laughter. 'Will you see that it's delivered?' McAuliffe asked, his broad face relaxed, although he knew now that he was challenging fate. 'After all, by the time the Kraut commander gets it, the Fourth Armoured Joes will be in Bastogne.'

'Sure, General,' the Colonel answered, 'I'll deliver it myself. It will be a lot of fun!'

'*Nuts!*' General von Leuttwitz exploded, his coarse face flushing red, his monocle popping out of his right eye, 'what in three devils' name does it mean?'

'I don't exactly know, sir,' the Captain, who had brought McAuliffe's message back to 2nd Panzer HQ, replied unhappily. 'All they did was laugh when they handed it to me.'

'Is it affirmative?' von Luettwitz barked, controlling his temper with difficulty, the veins swelling out angrily at his temples.

'I don't think so. They looked very confident to me. All they did was laugh — and laugh.'

Von Luettwitz stared out of the open door of the barn to where his artillery batteries were beginning to go into position: gun after gun, nearly two hundred of all calibres. 'All right Captain,' he said thickly. 'We shall give them till sixteen hundred hours. If they don't surrender by then, we shall let them have the full weight of our artillery and air.' In sudden fury he flung the insolent American note onto the floor, and ground it into the dirt with the heel of his gleaming riding boot. 'Then we shall see whether *die Herren Amerikaner* are still capable of laughing so heartily…'

At virtually that same moment, back in Luxembourg, General George Patton was staring moodily out of the window of his office at the Hotel Alpha. Down below, the Boulevard Paul Eyschen was wreathed in thick fog, the people of Luxembourg moving through it like sad, grey ghosts. The fog had come creeping in just after dawn and curling itself around the HQ like a great silent cat, it had settled down comfortably, oppressing the staff officers with its grey gloom.

Slowly Patton turned and walked over to his desk. He picked up the phone and called Major Fuller, Ninth Air Force's weather expert. 'Fuller,' he asked, 'what's the latest reading at your end?'

'I'm sorry, sir. But for the next few days,' the expert answered, 'there will be unrelieved gloom. No break can be expected until about 26th December.'

'That means no ops for four days,' Patton said tonelessly, his heart as heavy as stone.

'I'm afraid it does, sir. We can't fly in this kind of weather. The Ninth Air Force is definitely socked in,' the expert concluded with a note of finality.

'Thank you.' Patton lowered the phone and stared into nothing. Chaplain O'Neill's goddam prayer hadn't worked. The Fourth Armoured wouldn't reach Bastogne this day!

CHAPTER 3

'Shit and goddam shingle again!' Triggerman cursed. 'Ain't there nuthin' else in them lousy, crappy food packs!'

'You can have a bit of my spam, chum,' Limey said cheerfully, spearing the piece of hot, dripping spam on the end of his bayonet and spreading it over the K-ration cracker.

Triggerman looked at him sourly, his dark face pinched with cold, as he crouched round the earth and gasoline fire on which the crew of Old Baldy were cooking their evening rations. 'You know what you can do with yer goddam spam, Limey?' he growled.

'Can't mate,' Limey answered without rancour, 'I've got a London Transport double-decker up there already!'

'Eh?' Triggerman looked at him blankly, the stewed beef dripping from the edge of his cracker unnoticed.

Limey shook his head in mock sorrow. 'Cor stone the crows! You Yanks don't have much of a sense of humour. Hey, and watch yer shit,' he pointed to the cracker Triggerman held in his dirty frozen hand, 'it's dripping from yer shingle!'

Triggerman jumped up from the tree stump with a curse. As the other T-Force men crowded around the flickering blue fire, grateful for its poor warmth, Limey finished the rest of his spam and wiping his greasy hands on the back of his pants began to clamber up the tall pine next to Old Baldy to continue the job of stringing a radio aerial.

T-Force was camped at the edge of a forest on the side of a ridge where the wind had stamped out huge hollows, as if some giant had bitten them out. Taking advantage of the cover, the weary frozen men were cooking up the first hot meal, poor thing that it was, that they had eaten in the last forty-eight hours. All day long they had zig-zagged along the edge of the River Sure, trying to find a ford or a bridge. But without any luck. The river was in spate and even if they had been able to get the strongest swimmers across, the vehicles would have had to remain behind. Once they had spotted a bridge through the driving snow. Excitedly they had twisted and turned down a series of snow-blocked farm tracks and trails towards it; but they had still been half a mile away from it when a Focke-Wulf 190 had come roaring in at tree-top height and destroyed the little wooden structure with its first bomb. Fortunately for them, the snow had closed in again just at that moment and they had escaped without being detected. Now the T-Force men rested while Limey, the outfit's most skilled operator who had learnt his trade with the 8th Army in the desert, tried to raise Patton's HQ for details of the 4th Armoured's push and new instructions.

Hardt squatted on an ammunition box, sipping the bitter black GI coffee and nibbling a cracker, smeared with cold egg and ham paste, listening to the German gunfire in the distance and watching Limey's skilled movements as he slung the aerial wire across the tall pine's snow-covered upper branches. Almost since the start of the operation, the Krauts had drowned Old Baldy's radio with German brass band music and Glenn Miller played at full blast. Perhaps now the little cockney might get lucky and be able to raise Luxembourg.

'Penny for your thoughts, skipper?' van Fleet asked suddenly, continuing to sharpen the blade of his knife on the instep of his combat boot — up and down, up and down — over and over again, as if it were of utmost importance.

'Penny for my thoughts?' Hardt echoed his words, his cold pinched face wreathed in the steam rising from the aluminium canteen. 'I don't think they're worth that much, Clarry.'

'Pretty blank at the moment, Skipper?'

'Yep. I feel like Colonel Koch back there in Nancy when he said he felt as if he were blindfolded and in a dark cellar, waiting for some joker to come up and give him it with a knife — where it hurts.' He indicated the west with a jerk of his head. 'Our guys obviously got to Bastogne before the Krauts. You can tell that by the gunfire. It's been going all afternoon.'

'Sure, I'll buy that, skipper. But they don't sound like our guns.'

Hardt nodded morosely. 'Yeah, I agree. They're Kraut okay. So you can conclude whoever got there from our side wasn't armed with heavy hardware.' He shrugged. 'Probably some scratch outfit they pulled out of a reinforcement centre.'

'Could be, skipper.' Clarence van Fleet ceased his stropping and tested the edge of his dagger with a cautious forefinger. His eyes gleamed with sudden satisfaction at what he felt.

'At all events you can bet a plug nickel to a silver dollar that it ain't General Patton's boys who are up there in Bastogne. And that's what's worrying me, Clarry.' He put his canteen cup down. The snow hissed and melted all around its hot base. 'Where in all hell's name is the Fighting Fourth?'

Exactly five minutes later Major Hardt had an answer to that question. Seated back in the half-track, Limey suddenly jumped up from his long-distance radio and pulled off his earphones. 'Major Hardt, sir,' he yelled urgently, 'I've got them ... I've got them!'

'Who?'

'*The Fourth Armoured* — they've been trying to get us all day!'

Together the two officers doubled over to the halftrack, while the men around the fires stared at them expectantly, mouths bulging with food.

Swiftly Limey spelled out the message while van Fleet scribbled it down on the message pad. 'Big friend expects your visit... Rendezvous map co-ordinate...'

A minute later, while the rest of Old Baldy's crew crowded around the half-track, Hardt deciphered the message and read it to them in clear text. 'We've got to link up with the Fourth's point which is pushing north on the secondary road to Bastogne to the east of the main Arlon-Bastogne highway. According to this message from Div HQ, the road's clear.' He grinned at his men's unshaven, weary faces. 'General Gaffey says it's gonna be a walkover!'

'Famous last words,' Limey said softly, but nobody was listening to him at that moment...

'*A bridge!*' Hardt cried, as the half-track breasted the snowy hillside and they saw the little column of armoured vehicles lined up on the other side of the River Sure, '*Hot dog, they've got a bridge!*' he swung round excitedly to face Big Red.

But the NCO's expression did not change; it remained hard and suspicious. 'But what the hell are those guys stuck out on the road like that for, sir?' he breathed in exasperation. 'Brother, if Kraut air spotted them now, they'd be clobbered for sure.'

Hardt's enthusiasm at spotting the Fourth's point and the bridge beyond vanished as quickly as it had come. Big Red was right. There was something strange about the column; six Shermans and a handful of jeeps, each one occupied by stiff, unmoving figures. He could hear the vehicles' motors running. So why didn't they cross the vital bridge and disperse on the other side into the cover of the snow-heavy pines?

'Red, you're right. There's something fishy about the setup down there. Limey,' he snapped to the radio operator, 'signal the rest of the column to stop at the bottom of the hill and take up defensive positions.'

'Wilco, Major!'

'Wheels!'

'Major?'

'Drive her into that little track there and keep the engine running.'

As the ex-cabbie edged the six-ton half-track off the road and into the cover of the trees, Hardt turned to van Fleet. 'You're in charge of the column, Clarry. If anything goes — well, you know what I mean — aim for that bridge like a bat out of hell and take it! Clear?'

Van Fleet's hand slipped down to his dagger. 'Clear, sir.'

'All right. Red, Trigger and you, Dutchie, get your weapons,' Hardt ordered, 'we're gonna have a little look at what's with the Fighting Fourth...'

'What do those guys think this is?' Big Red exclaimed, as they advanced cautiously towards the end of the column, 'a Sunday school hayride with taffy apples and sody pop on —'

'Knock it off, Red,' Hardt commanded, pausing and cocking his head to one side. 'Can't you hear?'

From within the last Sherman there came the sound of some radio operator far, far away, calling, '*Little friend, why don't you read me... Little friend, why don't you read me...?*' over and over again.

Instinctively Hardt knew why the Sherman's radio operator did not answer. He shivered suddenly but not because of the cold. 'Come on, you guys,' he commanded, his voice abruptly very low, 'we'd better check them out!' Gripping his carbine more tightly, he advanced down into that awesome, brooding valley, heavy with the smell of death.

'Sweet Jesus,' Triggerman breathed, even his pugnacious temperament awed by the sight of so much death, 'they're all dead!'

Behind him Dutchie crossed himself hastily, his eyes round with fear.

Hardt stared at the three occupants of the jeep, sitting upright in their seats, their faces already turning black, like rotting cabbage stumps in some winter-abandoned garden, each one of them with his throat neatly slit. As if mesmerised, he thrust out a hand to turn off the jeep's engine.

Red's big hand, the knuckles white and split with frostbite, descended upon it before he could do so. 'Better not, sir!' he commanded.

'What do you mean?' Hardt's voice was low and muted with the shock of their discovery.

Gently, hesitantly Big Red released his grip and pointed to the nearest soldier, a fair-haired PFC with freckles. 'Look at his right leg, sir.'

Hardt followed the direction of his gaze. A small round cylinder had been wedged beneath the boy's khaki slacks. 'Butterfly,' his cracked, dry lips formed the word with difficulty.

'Yep, a butterfly bomb. Move him and you get the whole goddam works in your face.' Big Red spat in the scuffed bloody snow. 'For all we know, sir, the whole goddam lot of them is booby-trapped like that.'

'Christ on a crutch!' Triggerman whispered. 'Who would do something like that?'

'Yeah, and why?' Dutchie added his voice.

Big Red held up the rimless helmet he had found in the snow-filled ditch just beyond the Sherman. 'Can't you guess?' he asked.

'Kraut paratroopers,' Triggerman answered, recognising the helmet at once.

Big Red nodded solemnly and threw the helmet back into the snow.

'But why?' Dutchie persisted. 'Why set them up like this?'

Major Hardt knew the answer to that question, but he remained silent, his eyes — suddenly very hard and alert — staring at the darkening hills beyond the bridge. They were up there, he knew that now, up there, waiting for them to walk blindly into the trap.

CHAPTER 4

Steiner lowered his glasses, satisfied that the handful of paras dug in on the other side of the little bridge were perfectly camouflaged, and squirmed his way out of the snowy bushes from which he had been observing the *Amis* down below on the road. With a slither of snow, he dropped back into the hollow in which the bulk of his triumphant little force was hidden.

In spite of the bitter cold and their exhaustion, they were happy. It had been a bit of luck, picking up the American radio message like that; but a lot of patience and planning had gone into making the most of that stroke of chance. The ambush had worked perfectly. Now the bearded, dirty paras were enjoying the fruits of their victory. Their bellies were full of looted *Ami* rations, and with Todt's permission they were smoking the enemy *Camels* and sucking on the rich *Hershey* bars, a look of near ecstasy in their red-rimmed eyes. It had been many a month since they had enjoyed such luxuries.

Todt dropped his cigarette into the snow, with the casual grandeur of a millionaire letting fall a half-smoked Havana, and stamped it out. 'Well, sir?' he demanded.

With a sigh of relief, Steiner flopped down on a tree stump. 'Whew,' he breathed, 'I think my goldfish is beginning to limp!' Todt laughed sympathetically. They were all exhausted. 'I'll write to the Führer about it, sir.' His face hardened again. 'But the *Amis*, sir?'

Massaging his right foot through his shoes, Major Steiner explained what he had seen down below. 'They've got fires going like a lot of short-assed Hitler Youth out on a picnic.

You can see them for kilometres. And the officers are squatting on their nice fat *Ami* arses having a conference.' He reached out a frozen hand. 'Give me one of those, Todt. I need a smoke.'

Obediently Todt offered the Major a *Camel* and waited patiently until he had taken his first puff before asking his question. 'You mean they haven't attempted to cross the bridge yet, sir?'

Steiner shook his head. 'No, the Prussians don't shoot that fast, Todt. You ought to know that. First they'll have a little chat to decide what to do next.'

'But they'll cross?'

'Oh yes, they'll cross all right. By now they'll have got over the shock of the little reception we prepared for them. Slowly they'll be thinking of that possibility.' Steiner took a long, lazy draw of the American cigarette; it tasted heavenly after the coarse black Marhoka tobacco he had been forced to smoke these last months. 'Why shouldn't they? They've got the bridge for the taking, or so they think. Hell, it'll mean a medal for their commander and you know what that means for the officers and gentlemen of every army?'

Todt grinned suddenly and tugged at the end of his broken nose — he knew all right. Steiner grinned too, recalling abruptly the radio conversation he had with von Manteuffel earlier that afternoon. The Fifth Army Commander had run true to form like all generals. There had been the congratulations — 'Excellent work, Steiner, excellent!' The exhortation. 'You mustn't let me down, Steiner. Keep those *Amis* off my back, till I capture Bastogne!' The appeal to his patriotism. 'Remember, Steiner, the whole future of the Fatherland depends upon the success of this offensive.' The reward. 'Hold them for another forty-eight hours, Steiner and by the great whore of Buxtehude, I'll see the Führer awards you the diamonds!'

'*Klar, die greifen an,*' he resumed where he had left off. 'They'll attack all right. After all, that's what generals are there for — to bribe headstrong, brave young fools to sacrifice their lives for a bauble, a bit of tin and a fancy ribbon, worth all of five pfennigs!' In sudden disgust with himself, the war, the whole world, he spat his cigarette into the snow and watched it hiss to its death there, as if it were of some importance.

Todt, in his turn, watched the man he had served loyally these last five terrible years and told himself that the Major was about at the end of his tether: he had seen too much, done too much, suffered too much since that tremendous May day in the summer of victory, 1940, when the two of them had stood, bareheaded, blackened faced, on the top of the newly conquered Eben-Emael, laughing like two crazy schoolboys. But that was long ago — another age. He cleared his throat noisily. But when will they attack, sir?' he asked.

Steiner shrugged. '*Amis* are creatures of habit,' he lectured the big NCO, his voice normal again. 'They always do the expected — it's something to do with their assembly line society. A million years ago, one of their general staff base stallions must have decided that the best time to launch an attack would be at dawn. So, the result is that the *Amis* always attack at dawn. Down there they'll sit on their well-fed *Ami* arses, reading their textbooks on infantry tactics and then when it's dawn, they'll move in, probably with two nice, neat little infantry sections on each side of the road, as prescribed in the books.' He laughed. When he spoke again, his voice was hard and determined as of old. 'And believe me, Todt, we shall be waiting for them!'

'Great crap on the Christmas tree!' Todt responded with sudden enthusiasm. '*Won't we just, sir!*'

It was an unearthly cold. At forty miles an hour, the wind raced across the surface of the snow, lashing their faces with millions of razor-sharp snow particles. Icicles hung cruelly from the nostrils and eyelashes. But as they stumbled cautiously towards the bridge through the snow, Hardt was grateful for the wind, however brutal it was: it covered their approach very effectively. For he was sure the Germans must have sentries dug in among the thick firs on the other side of the Sure.

Behind them on the road, next to that terrible convoy of dead men, the fires still flickered red through the whirling white gloom. Hardt knew he was chancing an air attack by keeping them going; but he reasoned their light would lull any Kraut observer into a false sense of security. After all, who in his right mind would attempt an attack across the little bridge at this time of night and in such terrible weather?

Hardt moved a fir branch aside carefully, ducking swiftly, as its snow showered down.

'Watch it, sir!' Limey behind him whispered urgently. 'It's ruddy parky enough out here. Any minute now, I'm expecting me goolies to drop off.'

'Sorry, Limey,' Hardt whispered. 'Pass the word. Everybody to wait here. I'm going forward to the bridge now with Lieutenant van Fleet. Okay, Clarry, let's go!'

Clarry swallowed hard. The old sick taste of fear welled up inside him for a fleeting second; then he conquered it again, as he always did. 'I'm with you, skipper,' he whispered and as they moved out of the trees, Hardt caught a glimpse of silver — it was the Lieutenant drawing his favourite weapon, the razor-sharp dagger. Ducking his head against the driving snow,

Hardt told himself grimly that this night of all nights, Clarry van Fleet would certainly need it.

Hardt's muscles screamed with the murderous strain they were being subjected to. He gasped out with the sheer agony of it all. His arms felt as if they were going to rip loose from their sockets at any moment. He grunted, grateful that the noise of the foaming water down, fifty feet below, drowned any sound he might make, and prepared to make his next move. Behind van Fleet gasped. 'Skipper, aren't we there *yet?*'

'Hold out!' Hardt answered and threw himself forward one last time. His frozen hands, already numb and bleeding from the terrible effort of swinging — monkey-like — from steel rung to rung below the bridge, seized the spar, slipped, and held. For one long moment Hardt hung, there, his chest heaving frantically, with the water gurgling menacingly below. Then he let go and launched himself into space. He plunged up to his knee in the deep snow that lined the far bank. An instant later van Fleet landed at his side.

Together they lay there in the freezing snow, as if it were the warmest and softest of beds, relieved at last of that terrible strain on their arms and shoulders, gasping with relief. Then finally Hardt forced himself to rise, knowing that the Kraut posts could only be a matter of yards away. Van Fleet stirred himself, knife gripped in his hand once more.

Hardt put his mouth close to the Lieutenant's ear. 'Clarry, you break right ... I'll go left. With a bit of luck we'll come in behind them.'

'Roger, skipper.'

'And remember no shooting. There'll be more of them up on the height up there. We don't want to draw their attention down here until I've got the boys across.'

'Don't worry, skipper. The way I'll go about it, there'll be no noise.' He flashed the knife under Hardt's nose. 'You get me?'

'I get you, Clarry. Okay, here we go — and Clarry?'

'Sir?'

'Best of luck!'

'Thanks, skipper.' An instant later he had disappeared into the streaming white cloud of snow particles.

Cautiously Hardt started to circle the German positions. There was no sound, save the howl of the wind, an eerie elemental sound which made Hardt's hair stand up at the back of his neck. Twice he stopped and swung round, half-expecting a Kraut to loom up out of the white gloom behind him; but twice there was no one there. 'For Chrissake,' he whispered to himself angrily, 'get a goddam grip of yourself!'

Yard after yard he advanced on the snow-heavy bushes where he knew the Krauts must have placed their guards to watch the bridge, lifting and placing his foot down with the utmost care, as if he were walking across egg shells. Abruptly there was a low familiar hissing noise. He stopped immediately. In another place and at another time the most human sound of a man breaking wind would have been comic; here it was like a trumpet sounding a call to battle. He had almost walked into a German sentry!

Slowly, very slowly, Hardt sank to the ground and then twisting his head to one side, brought up his gaze from an angle, using the old, old trick to see better in the white darkness. Suddenly he stopped. A darker outline loomed up against the little heap of snow-covered branches which covered the hole he had dug himself in the ground.

With fingers that felt like swollen sausages, Hardt pulled the bayonet from his belt, stuck it in his teeth and started to crawl through the snow towards the first sentry. *Fifteen yards ... ten yards* … he could make out the pale blob of the man's face now, framed by the hood of his cape … *five yards*… He could hear the soft contented rhythm of the man's breathing. He was asleep … *three yards*… Hardt paused and taking the bayonet out of his teeth, grasped it firmly like a dagger in his right hand … *one yard*… He could smell that typical odour of Kraut soldier now, a mixture of sweat, black tobacco and garlic sausage. *Now*, a little voice within him cried. He hesitated no longer. With a grunt he dived forward. The German's face contorted with terror and agony, as the bayonet plunged deep into his chest in the same instant that he opened his eyes and saw his murderer for one fleeting second. A moment later he reeled back against the side of his foxhole, dead.

Slowly with a horrible sucking noise, Hardt drew out the bayonet. The German slithered to the bottom of the hole. Hardt licked his suddenly dry lips. He was trembling all over. But he knew he had to go on. There was no other way. Carefully he skirted the hole and began to crawl to the next position.

A matter of yards away, Clarence van Fleet stared transfixed at the German para, leaning against a tree straight in front of him. So far the Kraut, his cape covered in snow so that he looked like part of the bushes, had not seen him. But Clarry could tell from the little noises he was making that in a moment, the German would open his eyes and see him. Yet he was unable to move. He was rooted to the ground with sheer, naked fear.

The German opened his eyes. He stared at the man crouched in front of him in sheer absolute disbelief, as if this thing could not be happening to him. Slowly, incredibly slowly, he opened his mouth to yell a warning.

Suddenly the spell was broken for van Fleet. The knife hissed from his hand, almost as if by its own volition. The German threw up his hands to protect himself. Too late! The razor-sharp blade caught him directly in the throat. His yell died in a frantic gasp of pain. In that same moment van Fleet dived forward. He caught the German just as his knees began to buckle beneath him like those of a newly born calf. Gently, like a mother tending a beloved child, the American lowered the dying man to the snow and then with a savage grunt drew the knife out and plunged it brutally into the German's heart once more.

It was thus that Hardt found him, towering bent-shouldered over the dead German, arms hanging limp and ape-like at his sides, one hand clutching a blood-stained knife. But he had no time to question van Fleet's stance. There were other things to be done. 'Clarry, I got the rest. I'll hang on here. You double back and get the boys!'

Van Fleet shook his head violently, as if he were trying to wake from a deep, deep sleep. Then he answered in a voice that was strangely toneless. 'Okay skipper. Will do!'

Minutes later the rest of Old Baldy's crew were running silently through the streaming snow to where Hardt crouched among the dead German sentries. 'Hot shit, sir,' Red whispered gleefully, 'you pulled it off ... we've got a bridge!'

'Yes, Red, we've got a bridge,' Major Hardt answered, but there was no note of triumph in his voice as he stared down at the sightless eyes of the boy he had just murdered.

CHAPTER 5

The Americans attacked at dawn, as Steiner had predicted they would. But not where the big Major expected.

Abruptly the soft clatter of tracks across frozen snow awoke Steiner. There was a sudden soft crack. A flare hushed into the grey sky. It burst directly above the para camp in the hollow, bathing the startled Germans in its unreal, blood-red light.

'*What in the devil's name* —' Steiner began. The explosion of another flare drowned his words. And another. They came from all sides now, turning night into day. Steiner scrambled to his feet, machine pistol in one hand, arm held across his eyes to shield them against the harsh multi-coloured glare. The rumble of tracks was getting closer and he could hear the *Amis* yelling as they came up the hill.

'*Stand fast!*' he cried desperately.

'*Amis — they're all around us*' a panic-stricken para screamed. '*Run for it!*' The man dropped his weapon and started to run clumsily through the deep snow.

'*Stand fast, I say!*' Steiner bellowed.

But the panic was not to be halted now. Caught off their guard so completely, the paras broke, pelting for cover over the blood-red glowing snow, flinging away their weapons in their haste.

As if to lend speed to their flight, an *Ami* half-track breasted the rise. Immediately its gunner opened fire with his machinegun. Angry red-and-white tracer hissed flatly across the snow. A para threw up his arms melodramatically and dropped screaming. Another, hit in the back, faltered, staggered another couple of metres and flopped face downwards without a sound. Yelling hysterically the surviving paras blundered into the thick firs to the right of their camp, running right into the waiting T-Force men.

Steiner fired an angry burst from the hip, hearing the slugs patter on the armoured side of the half-track like heavy summer rain on a tin roof. But the vehicle kept rolling towards them.

'Look out, Major!' Todt yelled urgently.

He ducked. Just in time. The *Ami egg* grenade sailed over his head and exploded in the firs behind him. The thin trees came crashing down. Red hot splinters hissed through the air. Dirt and frozen snow pattered against his helmet.

Todt fired a burst from his Schmeisser. There was a scream of agony and the half-track came to a sudden halt. 'Sir,' he gasped, 'we've got to get out of here — *quick*!'

'But the men?'

'They've had it. Listen to that, sir!'

Steiner knew what the big NCO meant. The panic-stricken survivors of the surprise attack were being slaughtered in the bushes. There was no helping them now.

'It's every man for himself now, sir,' Todt put his own thoughts into words.

'You're right, Todt,' Steiner cried urgently, seeking for some way out while the enemy bullets whipped up the snow all around them, showering them with it, as if death itself were already trailing its icy fingers across their frightened bodies. 'But how?'

'Back up onto the heights?'

'Nix, Todt. That's what they're expecting. They'll be waiting for us,' Steiner said urgently. 'No, straight into the direction they came from. Through the *Ami* lines. That should take them off guard. *Come on*!'

A hundred metres away, the half-track had begun to move again. Its machine gun chattered. Tracer cut through the air. As they had been trained to do so long before, the two veterans rolled to the right. Once, twice, three times in rapid succession, leaving the enemy slugs to strike the snow harmlessly at the place where they had been a moment before. Then they were up, pelting down the snowy hillside towards the little bridge.

They clattered across it, bullets stitching a deadly pattern around their heels. An American loomed out of the gloom. 'What the Sam Hill —' He never finished his startled query.

Todt kneed him smartly. He went down, screaming through the vomit. Steiner kicked him in the face as he lay there writhing in agony. They ran on.

'Sarge, the bastards are escaping!' an angry young voice cried from the trees to their right. Steiner swung round, firing from the hip as he did so. An American fell out of the firs, his chest ripped open. Another came out of the trees, firing as he did so. Todt dived forward. The two of them went down in a crazy ball of flailing arms and legs. Todt let go of his Schmeisser. With both hands he seized the *Ami's* helmeted head and smashed it against the boulder protruding from the snow. The *Ami* screamed thinly. Todt grunted and forced the helmet down against the stone again — and again. Blood poured from the American's nose and ears in a thick, red, steaming, stream. His eyes rolled upwards. He was unconscious, perhaps dying. But Todt had been seized by a great atavistic anger, he would not stop. 'Come on, Todt,' Steiner yelled, grabbing him by the shoulder and tugging him free. 'Leave him — he's had it!'

Todt rose to his feet, shaking his head, a strange faraway look in his eyes. Steiner picked up the NCO's Schmeisser and flung it at him. Automatically he caught it. 'Come on,' he commanded, 'we're not out of the shit yet by a long way.'

They ran on. Ahead of them there was a bend in the snowy trail. Once they were round it, they would be out of sight of the *Amis* on the hill. Then they might have a chance. Steiner ran as he had never run before. At his side, Todt pelted forward, his big chest heaving crazily, as if it might burst at any moment.

There was the sudden high-pitched venomous hiss of an *Ami* machine pistol. '*Ach Scheisse!*' Steiner cursed and faltered as the burning pain ripped through his shoulder. The action saved both their lives. The second burst of *Ami* fire ripped the snow apart just in front of them. Todt reacted instinctively. His Schmeisser chattered into frantic, hysterical life. Swaying from side to side, he sprayed the bushes with slugs until his magazine was empty. An *Ami* came staggering out of the trees, bleeding from a dozen wounds. He croaked something they couldn't understand and flopped face downwards in front of them in the middle of the trail. They stumbled across his body and staggered on. Seconds later they were round the bend and blundering blindly into the trees and safety.

The hoarse enraged cries of the Americans had long died away. Now the two survivors of the ambushed paras plodded doggedly through the deep snow of a firebreak in the forest. There was no sound save that of their own harsh breathing and the stomp of their boots on the snow. Steiner estimated that they must have put at least four kilometres between themselves and the Amis, yet he still continued his southerly course with the aid of the compass strapped to his right wrist, in spite of the fact that he knew it was taking them deeper and deeper into the enemy lines.

'When are we going to break east, sir — back to our troops?' Todt gasped finally, posing the question he had been expecting for some time now.

Steiner held up his hand and leaned against one of the firs. Gratefully Todt followed his example. 'Listen Todt, I'm not ordering you to do this — I'm asking you as one comrade to another. Clear?'

'Clear.'

Steiner wiped his crusted lips with the back of his dirty, blood-stained hand and hesitated, as if he did not know exactly how to begin. Then he drew a deep breath and plunged in. 'You know what I said about medals last night?'

Todt nodded but said nothing.

'Well, men like you and me don't fight for shitty trinkets like that. We don't fight for Führer, Folk and Fatherland either. If we ever believed in such things, it was a damn long time ago, yes?'

Again the big NCO nodded, but said nothing.

'So what keeps people like us going, after all we've been through?' Steiner answered his own question. 'I'll tell you,' he said through suddenly gritted teeth. 'Because we believe in ourselves, because we believe in all the good men who died at our side for the same belief, because we're the paras — *paras of the old Seventh.* Do you think all those good lads who bought it in Holland in '40 or Crete in '41 would have given up because there were only two of them left?'

Todt's eyes began to glow again with their old fire. 'You mean, sir, you want to go on?'

'Right. I don't know exactly what we can do to stop the *Amis* pushing for Bastogne. There are only two of us after all. But we can do *something!* Another couple of kilometres and we'll be in their rear area, filled with fat-arsed base stallions, who don't know one end of a rifle from the other.' He grinned suddenly. 'Easy pickings for a couple of hairy-arsed old paras like you and me, Todt, eh?'

The grin was infectious. Todt beamed at the Major. 'You don't have to ask, sir, I'm with you... It'll be like in the old days, *march or croak*!'

'*March or croak it is, Todt*.'

With new energy the two paras started to march southwards again, their shoulders squared like the veteran soldiers they were. A few moments later they disappeared down the trail. But T-Force had not seen the last of Major Steiner yet...

PART FOUR: STALEMATE

'Gentlemen, there is a species of whale, which spends most of its time down at the bottom of the ocean, I am told. At this present moment, I feel a helluva lot lower than that whale's arse!'

General Patton to the Staff of the 4th Armoured Division, December 24th, 1944.

CHAPTER 1

In the sudden sun, the battleground glittered with hoarfrost. Now the grey began to disappear leaving the morning sky a hard, brilliant blue. In their foxholes, the weary paratroopers of the 101st Airborne stopped massaging their frozen feet and turned their bearded faces upwards to catch the slightest warmth. Here and there a paratrooper chanced his luck by clambering stiffly out of his foxhole to urinate on the frozen ejector of his M-I to thaw it out.

Back in the beleaguered town of Bastogne, the HQ staff started to stir. Under a guard of paratroopers, ragged greyfaced German POWs began to hack at the frozen earth to make the graves the 101st required this morning of the 23rd of December. Waiting for them on the side of the rutted, shellpitted road were a couple of dozen dead paratroopers, frozen into the ghastly postures of the violently done to death: mouths agape, limbs bent at impossible angles, shocked, vacant eyes staring unblinkingly at the sun.

But the group of staff officers now gathering outside the 101st Command Post were not depressed by the sight of the night's batch of dead from the hard-pressed division. Indeed their thin pinched faces were bright and happy and they kept making mysterious quips to each other about 'pennies from heaven'. When questioned why, they would glance up to the hard blue sky, wink knowingly and advise the mystified questioner to 'wait and see'.

At 9:35 precisely, the waiting staff officers' patience was rewarded. They forgot their frozen feet and ears. All eyes swung to the west as the sleek fighters came barrelling in —

silver fish in a blue sea. McAuliffe counted them and breathed, 'Gentlemen, there are sixty of them!' His officers cheered.

Suddenly the P-47s dropped their wing tanks which had brought them all the way from England. The action served as a signal. They broke formation. While the paratroopers stood up in their foxholes and cheered them madly, the fighters swarmed to the attack. Rockets hissed from their wings like a flight of angry red hornets. Bombs followed, exploding in balloons of orange flame and black smoke, which spread soundlessly, brilliantly, over the dazzling white hills surrounding Bastogne. As German tank after tank went up in flames, the enemy infantry cowered at the bottom of their shaking trenches, hands clasped over their ears, drowning out the steady drone of the approaching armada.

'*Here they come, fellers!*' the cry went up.

Around the bare slope which ran from the red-brick headquarters towards the edge of town, the waiting jeep drivers started their engines. They were the recovery teams. As soon as the drop started, they would start gathering up the urgently needed supplies and deliver them directly to the line outfits.

The first sixteen Dakotas knifed in from the west in perfect formation, brilliant white vapour trails streaming out behind them in the icy blue sky. The German flak opened up with a roar. Suddenly the sky was pocked everywhere with balls of black smoke. Still the transports kept on coming. The first plane was hit. It seemed to falter in mid-air. A wing broke off and came fluttering down to the ground like a great silver leaf. There was gasp of horror from the spectators. An instant later the plane exploded in mid-air.

A second one was hit. Bright scarlet flame began to lick around the starboard engine. The pilot feathered it. To no avail. Slowly, inevitably, the C-47 curled up on its port wing and nosed down in a terrifying vertical dive, white smoke pouring from its tail. The horrified watchers could visualise what was happening up there. They had ridden often enough in such planes. Two terrified Army Air Corps kids fighting the controls with sweat-soaked hands, the cockpit window showing nothing but a crazy whirling mass of up rushing earth. The plane hit the ground and crumpled up like a banana skin.

But still the others came on. Plane after plane, sailing through the shell-pocked sky majestically, as if unaware or contemptuous of the flak. A hundred of them ... two hundred ... two hundred and fifty.

Below, the signal fires flickered on. The dispatchers reacted immediately. Bundle after bundle came tumbling out of the Dakotas' open sides. In an instant the sky was ablaze with the bright red, blues and whites of the opening parachutes.

Suddenly the watchers awoke to the significance of the drop. As the jeeps raced out across the snowy DZ to collect the precious supplies, bearded paratroopers embraced each other, their eyes shiny with tears. In the streets of the battered little town, GIs and civilians danced together. A bareheaded little soldier, with a blood-stained bandage around his left hand, thrust his way through the crowd of excited staff officers grouped around McAuliffe and stuck his good hand out. 'Gimme five, General!' he ordered. 'Now we'll beat the Krauts for sure.'

Obediently the Commander of the 101st Airborne gave him his 'five'.

Patton was jubilant about the weather. While the sun streamed down outside and the happy-faced civilians stared up at the hard blue sky, once again full of American planes, he called Colonel Harkins to his office. 'Goddammit, Harkins,' he exclaimed happily, a big smile on his thin face. 'Look at the weather! That O'Neill sure did some potent praying. Get him up here. I want to pin a medal on him!'

Grinning broadly, Harkins went out to fetch the Chaplain. Some time later a bewildered O'Neill was ushered into the Commanding General's office. Patton sprang to his feet. With his right hand outstretched, he crossed the room to meet an embarrassed O'Neill. 'Chaplain,' he announced heartily, 'you're the most popular man in this Headquarters. You sure stand in good with the Lord and the soldiers.' Patton took the little medal from its case and pinned it on the surprised Chaplain's chest. O'Neill looked down and could hardly believe his own eyes. General Patton had just awarded him a combat decoration, the Bronze Star!

But after the bewildered Chaplain had gone 'back to Tabernacle', as Patton had cracked to a grinning Harkins, the General's happiness vanished. The news which had begun to come in from 4th Armoured HQ was not good. Its Combat Command A had been stalled by a destroyed bridge over the River Sure at Martelange and could not move until the engineers managed to throw a Bailey bridge across; and Dager's Command B was making terribly poor progress, moving forward at a snail's pace.

Just after midday, Patton received a direct message from McAuliffe. The paratroop commander thanked him for the supply drop, but added pointedly: 'Expected to see you today. Disappointed. Please remember there is only one more shopping day to Christmas!'

The message reminded Patton of his promise to Eisenhower at Verdun that he would be in Bastogne by Christmas. Now he had exactly thirty-six hours left to keep that promise. The knowledge spurred him into action. He called Gaffey. The harassed 4th Division commander was embarrassed and apologetic. But Patton had no mercy. 'Listen, Hugh, I want Bastogne — and I want it fast! Tell Dager from me there's too much piddling about. Bypass those goddam towns! he snapped angrily. 'Clear 'em up later. Tanks can operate off the roads now. The ground's okay. Hugh, I'm relying on you. Get on the ball or take the consequences.' The threat was obvious. As Gaffey put down the phone, he knew instinctively that if he did not take Bastogne soon, His days as Commander of the 4th Armoured Division were numbered. Almost sadly he picked up the phone again to call Dager.

Patton was not the only impatient Commanding General that glorious December day. Flushed and angry, an unusual state for the normally self-controlled von Manteuffel, the undersized Fifth Army Commander faced an unhappy von Luettwitz. 'I'm not asking for explanations, von Luettwitz,' he snapped, 'I'm asking for results!'

'But as I told you before, General,' the Corps Commander said, 'I just don't have the infantry to take the damned place.'

'And as I told you before, von Luettwitz, you don't need infantry. You need fire-power and when that has done its job, you use your tanks. We did it in France in '40 and in Russia in '41.'

'But those men in Bastogne are not frogs, nor Ivans, sir. They are *Amis*, sir.'

Von Manteuffel clicked his tongue impatiently. He knew von Luettwitz of old. In spite of his gross appearance, he was careful with his men, perhaps too careful. He did not like to take casualties — and it made him hesitant. 'Now, listen, von Leuttwitz,' Manteuffel rapped, restraining himself with difficulty, 'my point is within sight of the Meuse. I don't believe in the Führer's completely unrealistic objectives for this offensive. I know and you know, we shall never reach Brussels! But if we can establish bridgeheads on the Meuse, we can swing north and roll up the whole US 1st Army, perhaps even their 9th Army. Then, my dear General, the Allies might be prepared to talk peace and leave us to deal with the Ivans in our own time.'

Von Leuttwitz nodded his understanding. Now he could understand the little Army Commander's determination and impatience; he really did believe that there was some value in what he, von Luettwitz, had thought all along was a mad gamble, for which it was not worth throwing his men's precious lives away. It had been for that reason he had hesitated to attack the previous day and had attempted to fool the obstinate *Ami* paratroopers into surrendering.

'But I need Bastogne, von Luettwitz,' von Manteuffel continued urgently. 'I can't leave it in enemy hands to my rear. It would endanger my whole plan.'

'I understand, General,' von Luettwitz exclaimed, warming to his Army Commander's fervour and drive.

'Tomorrow I expect a heavy *Ami* attack from the American cowboy, Patton to the south. But I am prepared for it. Thanks to the self-sacrifice of *some* of my troops,' he looked pointedly at the Corps Commander, 'who undoubtedly have given their lives to buy me time, that lame-arsed Fifth Para Division has finally arrived in the line to your south. They will take care of Patton.' He shrugged. 'But for how long, that is the question — twenty-four hours perhaps, no more!' He rammed his cap down on his shaven head. 'And that is exactly the time I'm giving you to take Bastogne, General — *twenty-four hours.*' He looked grimly at the other man with his gimlet-eyes. 'General von Luettwitz, you will capture the town of Bastogne for me by this time tomorrow night, or you must be prepared to accept the consequences, unpleasant as they will undoubtedly be. Now may I wish you goodnight.' A moment later Manteuffel marched out, leaving the Corps Commander staring blankly at his situation map, crowded with red and blue crayon marks that marked the comings and goings of unsuspecting men, who would now have to conquer or die soon...

Two miles away in Bastogne, with a brilliant moon illuminating the besieged, silent town in its icy glare, McAuliffe's staff officers were celebrating a premature Christmas Party. McAuliffe, now sound asleep, had already warned them that 'Christmas Eve is a big deal for the Krauts. They get all mushy and sentimental about it and you can bet your bottom dollar they're going to try their damndest to give this place to their Führer as a present tomorrow.' The officers had taken the statement as a warning. Now they celebrated in the tight, stuffy blacked-out room. There was swing music from London, looted Belgian schnapps and cheap German cigars, found in a shot-up enemy truck the day before.

Drunkenly a full colonel staggered to his feet and said thickly: 'The Queen!'

Solemnly the officers got to their feet and raised their glasses.

'General Eisenhower!' Again glasses clinked.

'Marshal Stalin...'

'Lady Macbeth!' They giggled uproariously and stumbled up once more.

But as the evening progressed and the fiery plum brandy began to take its effect, their bumptiousness disappeared to be replaced by a brooding melancholy. Softly, the harshness gone from their drink-thickened voices, they began to sing the old carols of what seemed another age.

It was midnight when they reached *Silent Night*. Suddenly in the middle of the second chorus of *'silent night, holy night,'* there was a steady powerful hum from the east, growing louder by the instant. The words froze on their lips. All around them the windows — or what was left of them — had begun to vibrate violently. Slowly, very slowly, like puppets worked by some incredibly ancient puppet master, the officers started to turn their heads to the direction of the sound.

'Sounds like bombers,' a staff captain breathed.

'Ours?' another man queried. He attempted to laugh but failed miserably. 'That guy Patton must really be riding those 9th Air Force boys to make 'em come out this late —' The words froze on his lips. A thin whistle had split the silence outside. It grew louder and louder. There was no denying the menace of that sound. '*Krauts!*' the staff captain cried frantically and flung himself to the floor in the same moment that the first German bomb exploded in Bastogne.

As the full weight of the German air attack descended upon them, setting the floor beneath them heaving violently and the plates rattling on the wildly swaying table, the cries of alarm went up on all sides. '*Stand to ... stand to everybody ... the Krauts are attacking all along the line!*'

Madly the staff officers, their drunkenness vanished, grabbed their helmets and pistols, and ran outside into the burning, chaotic darkness.

Behind them in the suddenly empty room, the candles on the pathetically decorated Christmas Tree continued to glow a little longer. But one by one they guttered and went out altogether until the room was in darkness.

It was Christmas Eve, 1944...

CHAPTER 2

'*Okay, driver, roll 'em*!' Major Iryzk, CO of the 9th Tank Battalion, pressed his throat mike and commanded.

Below in the lead Sherman's driving compartment, the driver, narrowing his eyes against the sun's slanting rays, pressed the starter button. Immediately the tank's 400 hp sprang to life. Blue smoke shot from its exhaust and fogged the icy morning air.

As tank after tank of Combat Command B's lead battalion roared into noisy activity, shattering the country stillness, sending the black crows squawking in angry protest from the skeletal trees, Iryzk took in the village to his front.

Chaumont lay at the bottom of a bowl, the sides of which were formed by densely wooded hills, still deceptively silent. For all he knew they were full of Krauts, just waiting for them to come in and be slaughtered. Hastily he dismissed that unpleasant possibility from his mind and concentrated on the task at hand. While he took the lead companies to left and right of the village, his rear company would barrel straight for Chaumont. They would clear the main street for Hal Cohen's 10th Armoured Infantry Battalion, which would have the job of cleaning up for them. Meanwhile he would direct his lead tank companies through the fields to both sides of the village and outflank it and the hills. The skinny tank commander frowned. He knew he was chancing his arm by taking a bunch of thirty-ton tanks through those fields, still sparkling white with hoarfrost; all the same he knew that Patton had ordered General Dager to get off the road, and as Dager had told him at the briefing, 'when Ole Blood an' Guts says jump, you jump,

116

fellers.' 'Yeah,' one of the CCB's officers had replied, 'it'll be the same old story, *his* guts, *our* blood!' ' They had all laughed, but not very convincingly.

Iryzk threw away his cigarette. With an air of finality, it spluttered out below on the wet ground, which was already beginning to thaw out rapidly. He pressed his throat mike. 'Driver,' he ordered, '*advance!*'

Behind the tanks there was an earth shaking roar, which drowned the roar of the 9th Battalion's engines into insignificance. With a hoarse, exultant scream the whole weight of the Combat Command's artillery sped over the Shermans to tear into the silent village. In a vicious anger, flight after flight of 105mm shells ripped the air apart. Their red-hot sighing became a scream — one continuous, monstrous scream. The Fourth Armoured Division's attack towards Bastogne was moving again.

Crouched in the green-glowing, buttoned-down turret, Major Albin Irzyk watched the village loom larger and larger in his periscope. Now the leading houses were on fire. But still the Long Toms kept firing. Nothing, he concluded, could live in that hell. Behind the long column of tanks, Cohen's infantry would be moving into the attack now. Suddenly confident that everything would go well, he pressed his throat mike, 'Okay, driver,' he commanded, 'move off the road — and into the fields.'

'Sir,' the driver's voice came back, metallic and distorted over the intercom, yet clearly worried. 'It's thawing fast in this sun. I don't know if —'

'You're not paid to know,' the Major interrupted him harshly, '*move it!*'

The intercom went dead. Below the driver whipped through half a dozen gears quickly. In bottom gear, he started to edge the metal monster from the gleaming road. They cleared the ditch easily. A moment later they rolled onto the potato field. Lead pattered against the Sherman's sides like heavy rain. The Germans were reacting at last. But that didn't worry the Major; the handful of Krauts who might have survived the artillery bombardment were Cohen's problem. Behind him tank after tank moved into the field. Swiftly they spread out in battle formation. Confident now, the 9th Tank Battalion began to roll by Chaumont.

Up in the hills, the green young men of the 5th Parachute Division watched them, their thin pale faces a mixture of fear and anger. Already the first *Ami* infantry were beginning to advance into the burning village, held by only a handful of their comrades, coming forward cautiously behind other tanks. When would the Mark IIIs of the 11th Assault Brigade, dug in on the side of the snowy hillside behind them, open up and stop the damn *Amis*, they asked themselves. *When*?

The first company in line abreast were passing the bloated body of a dead cow, lying in the middle of the potato field, its thin legs sticking upwards like a tethered balloon, when it happened. The Sherman to Irzyk's right sagged visibly and began to sink. Frantically the driver raced the big engine. Mud and stones flew everywhere in crazy profusion. Impotently the tank's tracks raced round. But they were without traction. The Sherman started to settle into the mud of the thawed out potato field. 'For Chrissake, man,' Irzyk yelled over the radio, 'take it easy ... *easy does it*! Now —' 'Sir,' another urgent voice burst into the conversation, 'I'm sinking too! The sonuva bitch just won't move!'

Sweating heavily with sudden apprehension Irzyk spun his periscope round. It was Lieutenant Held's 'Betty Grable'. Already the star's shapely, million-dollar legs, painted on the side of the Sherman, were beginning to disappear in the sudden mire. And 'Betty Grable' was not alone. 'Eight Ball' had also come to an abrupt halt, its track revolving in impotent fury as it began to settle in the mire. To its right, 'G.I.Jive' was grinding to a stop. '*Christ on a crutch!*' Irzyk cursed, '*everybody — get the hell outa this field before the Krauts —*'

The rest of his words were drowned by a well-remembered crack. The tank battalion commander flung a mad look to his front. A zinc-like light flared on the nearest hill. And another. Like the sound of a huge piece of canvas being ripped apart, the first 88 shell zipped flatly through the morning air, the white-glowing armour-piercing shell gathering speed tremendously at every instant. '*Kraut tank destroyers!*' Irzyk had just time to yell frantically and then the great overwhelming deluge of death descended upon them.

The first trapped Sherman was hit. Its gasoline engine jetted scarlet flame immediately. An instant later it exploded with a great roar. Its crew hurtled through the huge ball of ugly red and yellow flame like crazy human flotsam. Another Sherman, crawling determinedly through the flying mud, was hit in the right track. It flopped out in front of the tank like a severed limb. 'Give him another round up his arse!' the excited, sweating German Mark III commander yelled, jubilant at the rich targets offered on a silver plate below, '*without the Vaseline!*'

Again the 88 thundered. The AP shell whammed against the side of the stricken, helpless Sherman. There was the great hollow boom of metal striking metal. The Sherman shook violently like a ship suddenly running into a hurricane. Next instant the tank was ablaze with flames.

Desperately the trapped Battalion tried to fight back. But even if they had been able to manoeuvre, the Shermans' 75mms would have been useless at that range against the mighty German 88s. Tank after tank was struck. Frantically a couple of the American drivers attempted to turn their tanks. In their panic they smashed into each other. They came to an abrupt halt. Next moment they too went up in flames, as the remorseless German fire descended upon them. Now the terrified tankers abandoned the fight altogether. Screaming hysterically, their only concern to get away from that terrible, merciless fire, they scrambled out of the turrets of their stricken vehicles and began to run heavily over the ploughed field to the rear. It was the opportunity that the para machine gunners had been waiting for.

An angry stream of green and white tracer slashed across the village from the hills. Some of the tankers threw themselves in the mud and the gleeful paras could see their slugs strike the *Amis'* twitching bodies over and over again. Others tried to run on, throwing away their helmets and side-arms in their all-consuming, overwhelming panic. They didn't get far. Caught in mid-stride, throwing up their arms in wild extravagant gestures, spines arched with that exquisite agony of death, they were thrown to the earth on all sides, as if slammed there by a gigantic fist. Lieutenant Gniot, the only surviving officer of the Company A, already bleeding from a wound in his shoulder, grabbed the turret machinegun of his stricken Sherman and poured a wild enraged burst of tracer at the hidden German positions, yelling at the wild-eyed fugitives, '*Move it ... for God's sake, move it now, while I cover yer!*'

They ran on. Gniot swung his machinegun from side to side. But not for long. The paras concentrated their fire on him. Gniot screamed piteously as a cruel burst tore his chest apart. He slumped over the gun, finger still clutched on its trigger, knocking its muzzle upwards. In his death throes he still kept firing, the tracer pumping upwards harmlessly. Then it stopped and the last officer of Company A was dead.

For Major Irzyk, the death of the young Lieutenant acted as a signal. He knew that it was hopeless to attempt to move forward under such terrible conditions. 'Make smoke!' he yelled desperately over his radio to the survivors, 'in Christ's name, make smoke and let's try to get the hell outa here!'

The remaining tankers needed no urging. Everywhere there were the soft plops of exploding smoke cannisters. The clumsy black objects sailed through the air and dropped to the mired tanks' front. In an instant a thick, white concealing cloud spread over the field, and roaring away in low gear, showering mud and pebbles over the bodies of the dead and dying, the handful of tanks began their painfully slow progress back the way they had come. Combat Command B's attack on Chaumont had failed miserably. The road to Bastogne was still blocked!

CHAPTER 3

'Gentlemen,' Patton announced grimly, 'there is a species of whale, which spends most of its time down at the bottom of the ocean, I am told. At this present moment, I feel a helluva lot lower than that whale's arse!'

Nobody laughed. Nobody could. The situation all around them at the 4th Division's CP was too grim. Ambulances, their windows bearing the ominous sign 'Carrying casualties', were hurrying back and forth through the stinking, clinging mud of the Belgian village, taking the survivors of the shattered 9th Tank Battalion and 10th Armoured Infantry to the rear. Around a mud covered Sherman a couple of hollow-eyed tankers were smoking their cigarettes in bitter silence; but the watching staff officers could guess what was going on in the men's minds: Patton had let them down.

'All right, gentlemen,' Patton continued, striding across to the map tacked on the kitchen wall under the moth-eaten crucifix, 'the attack on Chaumont was a complete snafu. I repeat, a complete goddam snafu.' He glared aggressively at the 4th Division commanders, 'and who is to blame?' He jerked a thumb at his own chest. 'Me, George Patton, junior. I'm the guy who told you you could work tanks on those cruddy Belgie fields out there at this time of year. It was my fault!'

Gaffey breathed a faint sigh of relief. At least, he wasn't going to have to take the can back for this particular snafu.

'Okay,' Patton barked. 'I've bared my breast enough. Chaumont is history. Let's get on with the job.' He stabbed the map with his forefinger, as if he wished he could bore a hole through it. 'Combat Command A, still stalled at Martelange while those goddam fat-arsed canteen commandos of engineers build them a bridge.'

'But, General,' Gaffey began…

Patton held up his hand for silence. 'I don't want any justifications, any excuses, any apologies, Hugh,' he announced. 'I'm just making a plain statement of fact.'

'I see, sir,' Gaffey said lamely and told himself he wouldn't like to be the engineer officer in charge of the bridge-building detail at Martelange.

'Here at Chaumont, Combat Command B got a very bloody nose this morning — something I don't need to go into detail about. Okay, so the Krauts think they've got us pinned down. The two main arms of the Fourth Armoured are stalled, eh?' He savoured the words bitterly. Outside a coarse, beery voice was saying: 'Okay, if any of you fish-eaters wanna go to mass tonight, you'd better get ya names down with the head shirt. If you're Jewish, go and light yerself a candle!'

Patton smiled suddenly. 'The season of good-will to all men, eh?'

Abrams, the inevitable cold cigar stump clenched between his lips, laughed too. 'You ain't kidding, General,' he replied, as irreverent as ever, 'this year Santa Claus better get himself some armour-plated reindeer if he's gonna go up that road.' He indicated the highway to Bastogne.

'Yeah, Creighton, you're probably right there,' Patton said. 'Say, do you have any armour-plated reindeer in Combat Command Reserve?'

The tubby little Colonel took the cigar slowly out of his mouth, 'You mean, the CCR is gonna be *honoured* again, General?' Patton nodded slowly, showing his stumps of teeth. 'Yes, Creighton, I'm tapping you.'

Abrams gave a mock groan of honour and slapped his forehead with the palm of his right hand. 'Boy, am I lucky!' he exclaimed. 'Here we go again!'

'Yeah, here *you go* again.' Patton was businesslike now. 'Okay, here's the deal. We're gonna make a fresh start, sticking to the roads this time. There's gonna be no more Chaumonts. Your CCR, Creighton, will assemble southwest of Bercheux on the Neufchâteau-Bastogne highway. From there you've got twelve miles of road till Bastogne itself. How you make it, that's gonna be your problem, Creighton.'

'You mean I'm gonna be given a free hand, General?' Abrams asked.

'That's right son. George Patton Junior is going to keep his big nose out of this one. The only order I'm gonna give you, is to kick off your attack on the morning of the 25th — and hit the Krauts with all you've got.'

'*Wilco*!' Abrams cried enthusiastically. He admired Patton, but he didn't want the Army Commander breathing down his back all the time as he had been doing with Gaffey for the last forty-eight hours. He liked to make his own tactical decisions. 'Thank you, sir … but I've one request.'

'It is?'

'I want your T-Force! If I can pick my own route from Bercheux, then I'd sure like Hairless Harry doing my recon for me.' Patton beamed at the chubby, undersized tank commander. 'Okay, Creighton, you've got him.' He chuckled. 'Already.'

Abrams looked at him incredulously. 'What did you say, General?' Patton inclined his head to one side, pleased with the effect of his surprise. 'Take a look out there and tell me what you see, Creighton.'

Colonel Abrams followed the direction of Patton's gaze. A battered half-track, laden with weary unshaven men, was crawling into the entrance of the farmhouse which was the Fourth's HQ. 'Jesus H. Christ,' he breathed, as he recognised the officer standing in the half-track's cab next to the driver, '*It's Hairless Harry himself.*' He dropped his cigar onto the dirt floor and stamped it out with his combat boot aggressively. '*Now you're really cooking with gas, General.*' he cried.

CHAPTER 4

'It's Kickapoo juice tonight, fellers!' Wheels yelled excitedly as he burst into the big barn occupied by T-Force. 'I've just seen Red outside officer country, mixing up a big batch of it!' He stared down at the tired, unshaven men lying on their blankets on the dirt floor. 'Tonight, we're really gonna hang one on, fellers.'

'And for chow?' Triggerman queried.

'Nix S on S, you can be sure of that, Trigger,' Wheels answered, his thin little face glowing in anticipation, 'there's gonna be turkey and home fries with all the trimmings.'

'Wow,' somebody exclaimed, 'they sure must be fattening us up for the killing!'

'Yeah,' others agreed. 'You ain't shitting there, brother! Little ole T-Force is gonna get it again!'

Outside the bells were beginning to ring. Wearily Dutchie got to his feet and began to struggle into his equipment. 'Where you going?' Limey asked curiously.

'Mass. It's Christmas, you know,' Dutchie answered, slinging his rifle over his shoulder. 'Why don't you come along?'

'I'm not a Roman candle like you.'

'Don't matter. Everybody's welcome, you know,' Dutchie answered, thrusting on his helmet.

'Okay, why not, Dutchie? The pong of sweaty feet in here is bloody awful anyway.' He indicated the T-Force men rubbing their bare yellow feet to try to bring some life back into the frozen toes. 'Hang on, while I put on my gear.'

The church was crowded with shabby civilians and smelled of stale apples, stable manure and incense. Carefully Limey and

Dutchie stacked their rifles against the white-washed walls and propped their helmets next to them. Awkwardly the two of them stood there and listened to the long sermon in French, which neither of them understood. Outside there was the steady boom of the artillery in the distance and close by a machinegun fired at intervals. While Dutchie concentrated on the priest's words, Limey grew bored. His attention wandered. His eyes strayed across the battered wooden pews — the first ones filled with children, then a row of older boys, another of girls, all plain and poorly dressed, and finally the adults. Mostly the men were old and bent, worn down by decades of hard work on the land. But two of them were young, firm-backed and strong. Limey could not see their faces, yet he wondered why two so obviously fit young men were still here. Most of the young Belgians, he knew, had fled deeper into the little country once the Germans had attacked to escape imprisonment or recruitment into the German labour battalions.

Idly he pondered the matter. But then the service was over and his mind was suddenly full of Big Red's potent mixture of industrial alcohol, fruit juice and white wine. He dismissed the two civilians. Grabbing his helmet and rifle, he said, 'Come on Dutchie, get yer finger out, mate, we're gonna miss our share of Kickapoo juice!' They hurried out, followed by the press of citizens — and Steiner and Todt...

The attendance at the Christmas Eve mass had served its purpose for the two paras. They were warm again and Todt had managed to steal a couple of the Hershey bars piled up on a plate at the rear of the church, which the *Amis* had donated from their rations that afternoon for the local children. Now munching the rich milk chocolate and feeling the new energy, generated by the sugar, streaming through their tired bodies, the two paras, clad in the ill-fitting clothes they had found the night before in an abandoned farmhouse, wandered down the village's main street. On all sides they could see the tankers, cursing and sweating, up to their ankles in mire and snow, as they loaded and readied their Shermans for the push. 'They're moving out, Todt,' Steiner whispered.

'Clear, Major. Look at that line of Shermans over there. There must be a whole battalion of them. And you don't need a crystal ball to guess what their objective is going to be.'

Steiner nodded. 'Bastogne.'

The two of them turned into a side alley, its snow stained yellow with animal manure. Carefully Todt broke the last Hershey bar in two and handed one half to the Major. 'Here you are, sir,' he announced grandly. 'The last course of your Christmas Eve dinner, Major. You can imagine the carp, the potato salad and a nice bottle of Moselle.'

Steiner laughed. He took off the ragged, holed sock he was wearing as a mitten and was about to put the chocolate in his mouth when a thick, but pleasant voice said behind him, 'You guys hungry?... *Vous avez faim?*'

Steiner spun round. In the faint light coming from a chink in the blackout curtain of the house opposite, he saw a big black face. A sergeant was standing there, big hands on his fat hips, swaying slightly as if he were drunk. 'By the look of you guys you could use some chow. *Vous voulez manger?*' he added in his fractured French, and made the gesture of eating in the continental fashion. Steiner made an instant decision. '*Oui, oui*,' he said eagerly, falling into his role as a starving Belgian civilian easily — he was damned hungry anyway, and curious — 'nix eat long time.' The drunken soldier beamed at that. 'Say, you guys speak American as well.' He chuckled merrily, his fat jowls wobbling, 'Follow me, guys. We got chow — and we got something else special too.' Staggering slightly, he began to crunch over the hard snow down the lane. Steiner looked at Todt, winked and slapped his pocket in which his pistol was hidden significantly. Todt understood. He nodded back. Together, they began to follow the big man.

'I'm not gonna shit you, Hardt,' Colonel Abrams said, rolling his unlit cigar stump from one side of his mobile mouth to the other, 'it's gonna be right tough out there tomorrow.'

Hardt grinned wearily, his bald head gleaming in the bright white light flung by the hissing Coleman lamp. 'It hasn't been exactly a picnic for the last three days either. I don't think I've ever been so goddam cold all my life, Colonel — and I come from Maine.' Abrams nodded and sat down on the wooden kitchen table which was serving him as a desk. 'Sure, I know, Hardt. I guess you and your guys must be bushed. But I'm afraid you're still on the hook till we roll into Bastogne.' His broad face hardened and he clenched his teeth, as if he were about to bite through his cigar at any moment. 'And brother we're gonna do it.'

Looking at Abrams' broad, pugnacious face, Hardt knew if anyone could make the last dozen miles to Bastogne, it would be the undersized, aggressive tank colonel.

'Now then, the Old Man has given me a free hand on this, thank God. You know how he is otherwise, always trying to play the game from the touchline. But now it's my show — one hundred per cent. Okay. So this is what I'm gonna do. The fields are out! We're going to stick to the roads. Naturally the Krauts will know we're coming and concentrate on blocking our approach roads.' Abrams shrugged quickly. 'And that's exactly what I want them to do.'

'How do you mean, sir?'

'Well, you see Patton got it all wrong — but don't ever dare tell him I said that, he'd have me down to a buck-assed rifleman in no time flat. He saw this operation from the wrong angle. You know the old story, Hardt, about the difference between a pessimist and an optimist? The pessimist looks at a glass of beer and says miserably — "hell, my glass is half empty". The optimist does the same and says happily — "*why my glass is half full.*"' Abrams ran his cigar across his mouth again before continuing. 'Okay, well the Old Man thought like the pessimist — the Krauts could pin *us* down at every damned crossroads. But I'm looking at the problem like the optimist, we can pin *them* down and —'

'Side-slip,' Hardt beat him to it, excited at Abrams' plan, 'on to another road.'

'And another, pinning them down all along the line, Hardt, until we find one where they can't pin *us* down. Hell, they can't hold up the whole weight of the Combat Command at every crossroads can they now?'

Hardt nodded his agreement. 'So they'll be static and we'll be mobile!'

'Right. So what am I gonna do? I've collected every damn canteen commando I can lay my hands on — cooks, clerks, the oddballs in the battalion stockades, even those boys we've got attached from the supply line* and I've given 'em a weapon. Wherever we get stalled, I drop off a bunch of them to pin down the Krauts and move on, keeping my vets for the real one. Somewhere, we'll find a road block where they're not in full strength and then we'll be through them like a dose of salts on a cold morning.' He took the cold cigar out of his mouth and pointed it almost accusingly at Hardt. 'Major,' he rasped, iron in his voice suddenly, 'I want you to find me that particular road block.'

'Sir!'

'And listen, Hardt, make it snappy. Those Joes in Bastogne are not gonna last out much longer. Okay?'

'Will do, sir.' Hardt snapped, infected by the other man's contagious enthusiasm. 'You can rely on T-Force!'

Todt and Steiner sat in the middle of the black soldiers, a canteen cup full to the metal brim with fiery bourbon in one hand, a massive corned beef sandwich in the other. All around them the GIs enjoyed themselves without restraint. The cramped smoky room was full of their high-pitched laughter, wild giggles and hand-slapping happiness. In the corner a looted radio was belting out what Steiner had once learned to call, 'decadent black jazz'. Their new friend, who enjoyed the highly unlikely name of Washington Sherman Lee Jones, had left them now to take his turn in enjoying the favours of the big-bosomed Belgian blonde, whose massive breasts threatened to burst loose from her tight-fitting artificial silk blouse at any moment, and they could talk again. 'What do you think, sir?' Todt asked cautiously over the metal rim of his canteen cup. 'They're pretty drunk — we could take 'em easily, with one hand tied behind our backs.' Steiner smiled thinly and pretended to take a sip of the fiery bourbon, which the men had looted from a supply truck. 'Ungrateful bastard, aren't you, Todt,' he whispered without rancour. 'They feed your face, take you in out of the cold, and now you want to croak them.'

Todt shrugged carelessly.

Steiner looked at the happy, sweating faces all around him, enjoying their own time out of war, away from the white bosses, celebrating with stolen booze and a stolen woman, and wondered again how they could look upon this as their fight, when they were segregated from the men at whose side they had gone to war; when they were regarded as second-class citizens. Yet, as he knew from their new friend Washington Sherman Lee Jones, all of them had volunteered to go into the line as infantrymen on the morrow. Suddenly he dismissed the thought as irrelevant. He had other things to do than worry about the injustices of the *Ami* social system. 'No, Todt, we don't kill them — not yet at least. This is what we're going to do…'

Minutes later as Jones came across to them again, buttoning up his flies and muttering something about 'well, that sure did take a load off Mrs Jones' boy's mind', the plan was worked out, and in hesitant English, Steiner asked his favour of the grinning NCO.

'Sure, sure,' Jones answered easily. 'Anything for a friend and an ally. Now you guys, what about another corned beef sandwich?'

Slowly a heavy profound silence started to descend upon the village. In their billets the last of the drunks crawled into their blankets, tossed and turned for a few moments, trying to find the most comfortable position on the hard wooden floors, and finally drifted off into an uneasy sleep. Outside it was bitterly cold. In their foxholes the sentries shivered continually and stared up the road, gleaming like crystal in the icy-blue light of the moon. Above them the coldly glittering stars seemed infinitely remote and infinitely cruel, as they gazed down at the war-torn landscape. From far, far away at the German positions, carried intermittently by the freezing wind, they could catch the sound of deep voices singing '*Stille Nacht, Heilige Nacht*'.

Here and there a GI reached out a frozen hand across the lip of his foxhole and took that of his neighbour. 'Happy Christmas,' they whispered hoarsely, as if they didn't want to break that awesome midnight silence. 'Happy Christmas, Joe.'

But finally the singing died away altogether and the sentries huddled ever deeper into the collars of their greatcoats, praying fervently for the dawn and relief from the murderous cold; yet terribly frightened of what horror that new dawn would bring. Before them the road to Bastogne waited in tense evil expectation...

PART FIVE: BLACK CHRISTMAS

'Son, the finest Christmas present the 101st could get would
be relief tomorrow.' —
General McAuliffe, December 25th, 1944.

CHAPTER 1

'Jesus H, sir,' Big Red cursed, his broad face almost disappearing behind a cloud of his own breath, 'it's colder than a witch's tit out here!'

Hardt chuckled without enthusiasm. 'Don't worry, Red, it's gonna get a helluva lot warmer before this day is out.'

'You can say that again, sir,' Limey said, crouched behind the two of them in the open half-track, ready to transmit the order to move out to the rest of T-Force, lined up behind them in the cold shadows at the side of the road. 'This really would freeze the balls off'n a brass monkey!' He shivered violently. 'Cor stone the crows, am I frozo!'

'Hold yer water, Limey,' Triggerman growled sourly. 'You're not the only one who's goddam cold.' The murderous cold had dampened even his usual enthusiasm at the prospect of violent action.

Hardt looked at his men, smoking quietly in the pre-dawn gloom, hands cupped carefully over the glowing ends of their cigarettes. He felt for them. But there was nothing he could do about it. Colonel Abrams wanted the road opened to Bastogne and he was not going to be put off from his aim by the fact that the air measured twenty degrees of frost at the moment, and that every five minutes his men had to open and close the bolts of their rifles to prevent them freezing up.

Van Fleet crunched across to Old Baldy. 'Five minutes to go, sir,' he whispered.

Hardt glanced at the green glowing dial of his watch. 'Five minutes to go it is, Clarry.' He tugged at the end of his crimson nose and tried to pummel some life back into it. 'Remember,

Clarry, keep from bunching up. As soon as we hit trouble — and we will, that's for sure — take the nearest side street. Once they've got us bunched up and stationary, we're for the chop. Easy meat for those damn bazookas of theirs.'

'Roger, sir.' Van Fleet grinned in spite of the cold: the CO had given him the same advice twice already this morning.

The minutes ticked away leadenly. Behind Hardt, Dutchie began to whistle the latest Beverly Sisters' hit '*The Boogie-Woogie Bugle Boy of Company B*' between his teeth with monotonous persistence. To his front, a streak of tracer crossed the horizon and Hardt thought he could make out the hammer of a BAR. But, he told himself, that was somebody else's war; nothing to do with him. Big Red opened his flies and urinated over the side of the half-track. The hot yellow liquid hissed as it struck the snow.

A sudden hush. A dry crack. An instant later the green flare exploded to their front, illuminating their pale faces in its sickly unnatural light. Hardt snapped out of his reverie. It was the signal he had been waiting for. His hand came down hard on Wheels' shoulder. 'Okay, soldier, take her away!' he commanded. Wheels pressed the starter. The White scout car rattled asthmatically for what seemed an age. Then with a great roar, the engine burst into life. Wheels rammed home first gear. Rustily the half-track started to move forward. Behind it, vehicle after vehicle followed suit. It was six o' clock on the morning of December 25th, 1944. The last attack on Bastogne had commenced.

The dawn sky had begun to break up. Here and there patches of harsh deep blue had started to appear among the dirty white. It promised to be another fine, if murderously cold day. But Major Hardt, in the lead half-track, had no eyes for the sky. His gaze was fixed intently on the village in front of him. Behind him the rest of the T-Force vehicles had come to a halt, waiting for his decision, crouched in the snow like black metal monsters.

Hardt wiped his dry, scummed lips and took in the place for a second time. It was a typical Belgian village of the area: a collection of dirty white, slate-roofed houses, huddled around the usual Gothic church, the point of its steeple hanging to one side, obviously damaged by some stray artillery shell. Nothing moved in the place. There was not even the usual hysterically barking farm dog. The village seemed empty.

But he knew that couldn't be. With the clarity of a vision, he knew that anxious, angry eyes were already watching his every move. Up in the church steeple, their artillery observer would be crouched over his radio, whispering his instructions tensely to the waiting gunners. Somewhere behind the first row of silent houses, from whose chimneys no smoke came, the bazooka operators would already be placing the long ungainly weapon over their right shoulders, ready for the battle to come.

He nodded to Wheels. 'Okay, move her — nice and slow!' he ordered. 'Trigger, as soon as we get within range, give the steeple up there a nice long burst.'

'Sir!' the ex-Mafia man, crouched over the .5 machinegun, answered smartly.

Behind him, Limey whispered swiftly into his mike. 'Moving forward now, George Six… Moving forward now.'

Two hundred yards away, van Fleet in the lead half-track of the rest of T-Force waved his arm in a big circle three times to acknowledge that he had received the message. Slowly, spread out at intervals, the other vehicles began to follow.

The village loomed up ever larger. Behind Hardt, Trigger swung the 50 calibre from side to side. At Hardt's side Big Red and Dutchie tensed over their grease guns. There was no sound save the hiss of the wind and the clatter of their tracks over the frozen snow. Slowly Hardt began to believe that perhaps the village was not occupied after all — surely the Krauts would have opened up by now if they were in possession? 'Wheels,' he began, 'I want you to take her —'

'*Look out, sir. Panzerfaust!*' Big Red yelled in alarm.

Wheels saw the ugly black object wobbling clumsily towards the half-track, dragging a trail of fiery red sparks behind it, and reacted instinctively. With a curse he swung the wheel round to the left and then to the right again, as if he were fighting the five o'clock rush on Fifth Avenue back in his native New York. The half-track swayed from side to side alarmingly. Hardt felt the heat of the German rocket on his frozen cheek as it sailed by with inches to spare. Next moment it had exploded harmlessly in the snow behind them, showering the crouching T-Force men with snow and pebbles.

The bazooka bomb seemed to act as a signal. A ragged crackle of small arms fire erupted from the first row of houses. A Spandau screamed in high-pitched hysteria. Tracer cut the air, racing for the half-track at a mad rate. Lead pattered suddenly on Old Baldy's sides.

'Step on it, Wheels … give her gas!' Hardt screamed above the racket. Wheels needed no urging. Peering through the narrow hole of the armour plated windscreen, he surged forward. In that same moment, Trigger let the church steeple have a vicious burst of fire. A dark figure flung up his hands and dropped from the opening there with dramatic suddenness. A second later they were at the entrance of the cobbled village street, firing at the windows on both sides.

Behind them the first T-Force vehicle was hit. It skidded crazily, to stop with its shattered front axle hanging over a ditch, flames pouring from its engine. Frantically its crew bailed out and ran for the nearest truck. They never made it. The German fire concentrated on them. They were swept off their feet by it and crumpled to the snow. An instant later a T-Force half-track crunched over their bodies, its tracks suddenly a bold red. But van Fleet wasn't stopping for casualties. There was going to be no bogging-down on this one. 'Keep going — for Christ's sake keep going, driver,' he yelled fervently. He caught a glimpse of a pale young face under a rimless helmet to his right behind a bush and fired instinctively. A scream of agony and the face disappeared. But there was another para behind him. Desperately van Fleet fired again. Too late! The German stick grenade hurtled through the air and exploded under the half-truck's front axle.

The six-ton vehicle reared high in the air, like a wild horse being saddled for the first time. It came down again with a tremendous crash, the driver, his neck broken, his face a mass of sticky blood, slumped dead over the wheel. '*Bale out!*' van Fleet cried, his helmet gone, his face ashen with shock, '*Now!*'

The survivors needed no urging. As the enemy fire concentrated on the stricken half-track, they swung themselves over the vehicle's steel sides, pressing their bodies close to it so that they would present the smallest possible target. Together with the bare-headed Lieutenant, they ran for their lives, the German bullets stitching vicious patterns in the snow at their flying feet.

Up front, Hardt caught a glimpse of a rough and ready barricade across the road. Tucked in one corner there was the long menacing barrel of a German anti-tank gun. 'Trigger,' he bellowed. The little man at the 50 calibre needed no further order. He swung the machine gun round. It chattered angrily, the empty cartridge cases rattling to the half-track's metal deck in crazy profusion. The anti-tank gun's crew scattered on all sides. Trigger mowed them down mercilessly. But Hardt had seen enough. T-Force would never get through the village. 'Wheels,' he yelled, 'see that barn — move through it!'

Wheels spun the wheel round. With slugs whining and careening off the half-truck's metal sides angrily, it sped at thirty miles an hour for the worn, wooden door of the barn, hanging loosely by a great rusty hinge. 'Hold tight, everybody!' the little driver cried above the noise. 'Here we go!'

The half-track's blunt nose hit the door with a mighty crash. It splintered, planks of rotten wood flying everywhere. A big brown plough horse blundered into them and galloped whinnying with terror, outside. Chickens scattered in flying feathered panic. A couple of Germans in the green camouflage capes of the paratroopers were flung out of the hayloft to disappear screaming under Old Baldy's flailing tracks. The half-track glanced off the side of an ancient cart. It splintered and sagged to the ground. Another wooden wall loomed up out of the gloom. Wheels tensed over the wheel. The vehicle struck it with a resounding crash. It splintered and gave; it had been as rotten as the door. Behind Wheels, Dutchie crossed himself in hasty gratitude. If they had been trapped in the barn, it would have been curtains for them.

But there was no time for prayer now. As vehicle after vehicle of T-Force took the same way out, plunging through the burning barn to the open countryside beyond, the Germans dropped out of their hiding places and pelted after them. A jeep driver lost control of his vehicle and plunged into a huge bale of hay. The paras ripped him and his vehicle apart with their concentrated fire. Bits of his body flew everywhere, mixed with the suddenly blood-soaked hay. In the confusion another jeep didn't make it. It crashed into the wall and began to burn at once, its occupants screaming frantically as they tried to blunder out of the burning murderous confusion of the barn, their uniforms furiously burning torches.

Minutes later the survivors had all passed through the barn and were grinding their way up the steep trail which led out of the village to the north-west. Behind them the cries of rage and the crackle of small arms fire grew fainter and fainter until they died away altogether. Finally when he was sure that the Germans, who were obviously not motorized, were not pursuing them, Hardt ordered a halt and asked for a report on casualties. As Big Red doubled away to carry out his orders, Hardt turned to Limey, 'Okay, contact Colonel Abrams, Limey,' he commanded 'and tell him to send up a bunch of his canteen commandos to pin the Krauts down in the village. Tell him too it's too tough a nut to tackle with his present strength.'

'Yessir,' Limey answered smartly, wiping the sweat from his smoke-blackened forehead. 'Anything else?'

'Yeah, there is. Tell him T-Force doesn't know where the hell it is, but it's continuing on the same course. He'll be hearing from me. That's all.'

'Righto, sir.'

A moment later, Big Red returned with the details of the casualties.

'Three vehicles have bought it, sir.'

'And the men?'

Big Red frowned; he knew just how much the CO treasured the men of T-Force. 'Not good, sir. Five killed and fifteen wounded. One guy's missing.'

Hardt nodded his thanks. 'Okay, Red,' he said wearily. 'Let's roll 'em again.'

As Old Baldy recommenced its long slow climb into the snowy hills, Major Hardt did a quick calculation. There were about a dozen villages and hamlets between him and Bastogne now. If his casualty rate for each one was as high as at the last village, he would arrive at the beleaguered town with exactly the crew of one half-track left. *T-Force would not exist any more!*

CHAPTER 2

All that long twenty-fifth of December, T-Force zig-zagged back and forth along the Belgian third-class roads and farm tracks. Time and time again they bumped into the Fifth Para Division's road blocks, attempted to force them and when they failed, backed off and called Abrams to send them up more of his 'canteen commandos'.

Their progress was pitiful and costly. Now T-Force was leaving a blackened, burning trail of knocked-out half-tracks and jeeps behind them and the Red Cross half-track was filling up swiftly with severely wounded men. The cold grew in intensity too. In the Red Cross half-track the harassed, overworked medics were having to tuck the frozen morphine Syrettes under their armpits to thaw them out before they could plunge them into the wounded man's arm and give him the blessed relief from pain; and the bottles of blood plasma had to be placed under the White's hood in order to keep them in working order.

Everywhere the pitifully frozen soldiers were following Limey's tip — 'we used to do this just before we kipped down on the Embankment for the night in the old days —' and stuffing old copies of the *Stars and Stripes* between their sweaters and khaki shirts as insulation against the terrible cold. Regularly at half hourly intervals, each vehicle commander ordered his men to rub each other's noses and ears to start up the circulation again in the frozen extremities. Weapons froze up, lenses clouded over, windscreens became panes of sheer ice. Yet in spite of his men's suffering, Hardt knew there could be no let up. Bastogne was under severe attack. It couldn't last out much longer. T-Force had to find a way through for Colonel Abrams' CCR.

Doggedly, Combat Command R followed the trail blazed by Hardt. Bercheux was taken. Vaux-lez-Rosières was next. Hardt had warned Abrams to expect a lot of trouble from Ramonville, the village which followed. By now Abrams was beginning to get angry; there were still eight miles to Bastogne and the light had started to go. He ordered that the Belgian village should be given the 'treatment' and there was to be no further 'goddam pussyfooting around!'

Swiftly, as the harsh, cold-blue of the afternoon sky began to give way to the grey of evening, a company of Shermans lined up on the high ground outside the village with their 75mms trained on the silent houses below. Behind them four whole battalions of artillery levelled their cannon on the same target. 'Okay,' Abrams barked, rolling his cigar to the corner of his tough set mouth, '*Take it out!*'

With an earth-shaking roar, the massed guns opened up. The village disappeared under a frightening barrage of high explosive. Hastily a combat team of tanks and half-tracks, filled with armoured infantry, rattled down the slope towards the village. They knew they had to be in Ramonville before the barrage lifted. It would be slaughter if the Germans caught them out in the open fields to the village's front. Just as the last shell dropped into the burning village, they made it. The light tanks roared down the cobbled, battle-littered streets, firing to both sides, while the infantry leapt from their vehicles and sprinted from house to house winkling out the paras hidden there. By dusk the job was finished. Ramonville was taken and there were over three hundred German prisoners in Abrams' hands.

Abrams' tanks clattered on, but not for long. Two hundred yards beyond the village, the retreating para engineers had blown a huge crater in the road, and they had picked the site well. It was bordered by a small unfordable river which made it impossible for Combat Command R to detour. Angrily Abrams spat out his cigar when he saw it and the great stalled column of tanks and half-tracks lined up on the single road north behind it. 'Goddammit to heaven,' he cursed, 'will we never get to that darned place!' And his staff officers knew well what place he meant — *Bastogne*.

In Bastogne now, the cellars were filled with wounded and dying soldiers and frightened, starving Belgian civilians. General McAuliffe had just completed his daily tour of the cellars when the telephone rang and he was informed that the Fourth Armoured relief column had been stopped yet once again. He sat there, numb and silent, ears not taking in the new German divebombing attack above. Down below him in the great seminary cellar, heavy with the revolting stench of human excrement which no amount of carbolic acid could counter, the civilians were already beginning to go mad with the almost unbearable strain; and already some of his younger men were starting to die in their foxholes without a trace of a wound on their bodies. They had simply given up the ghost and willed themselves to die.

'General,' timorously an aide broke into his bitter reverie.

'Yes?'

Cautiously the pale-faced aide handed him a roughly mimeographed sheet of paper. 'I thought you'd like to see, sir. We're handing it out to the whole division at chow time this evening.'

Blankly McAuliffe, the strain of these last terrible days evident on his broad, once good-humoured face now, stared at it, as if his eyes could not take in the words. Then he shook his head and forced himself to read the words. 'We are giving our country and our loved ones at home, a worthy Christmas present and by holding Bastogne we are truly making for ourselves a merry Christmas.'

For what seemed a long time General McAuliffe did not say anything. Finally he let the scrap of paper drop to the floor. 'Son,' he said to the aide in a hollow voice, 'the finest Christmas present the 101st could get ... would be relief tomorrow morning...'

In the end Hardt was forced to halt. T-Force had been on the move for ten hours now, fighting and retreating, twisting and turning down the murderous, snow-bound Belgian farm tracks without a bite of food, without even an opportunity to relieve nature. Looking up at the leaden sky, Hardt knew that if he didn't stop soon, it would be too dark to allow the men to make a quick fire and warm up a can of hash and a canteen of coffee. 'All right, Limey,' he ordered, 'tell the rest of the column to halt. We're gonna have a fifteen minute comfort stop.'

In spite of the miserable cold, Limey was irrepressible — as usual. '*Comfort stop!*' he cracked and shook his head in mock disbelief. 'Gawd, ain't you Yanks the fancy ones! In the old British Kate Kamey, we used to call it "piss and puff stop!"'

Hardt forced a weary smile. 'Get on with it Limey, willya?'

Stiffly, unable to feel their feet as they dropped to the snowy ground, the T-Force men urinated with sighs of grateful relief and set about getting their cooking fires going. Cracker tins were filled with frozen earth, doused liberally with gasoline from jerry cans and set alight. Swiftly they dropped cans of hash into the flickering blue flames, thrust pieces of spam, speared on the end of bayonets into them or held canteen cups of snow over the primitive, if effective fire, to make water for coffee.

Hardt was too tired to even move out of his seat and warm his frozen hands at the nearest fire. 'Jesus, Clarry,' he said wearily, 'I feel colder than a well-digger's ass!' He shivered dramatically. 'I have never been so goddam cold in all my goddam life — and I hope never will be again.'

Clarence van Fleet nodded. 'I know well whereof you speak, skipper,' he said, feeling he had never seen Hardt so worn and weary in the two years they had served together. 'Compared to my *derrière*, a polar bear's ass must be like an oven! And I'm wearing fleece-lined drawers!' Hardt chuckled throatily. 'I wish I were, Clarry.' With an effort of will he pulled himself together and unfolded his map for the umpteenth time that long miserable day. Poking a finger that felt like an over-stuffed German sausage at it, he said: 'We're about six miles from the Bastogne perimeter now, Clarry. Now as you know from Colonel Abrams' radio message half an hour ago, he's stalled again outside Ramonville.'

'Yeah, and I sure wouldn't like to be his long suffering exec, at this particular moment, skipper!'

'Agreed. The Colonel's temper isn't very good at the best of times, and by now it must have reached boiling point.' Hardt dismissed Abrams. 'Now you can see from the red marks on the map that most of the Kraut positions we've hit today seem to be to the left of the Neufchâteau-Bastogne road. Obviously they're not only screening Bastogne, but also their Panzers heading for the Meuse beyond Bastogne.'

'It certainly looks like that to me too, sir,' Van Fleet agreed.

'Okay, can't we assume that the Krauts will have fewer troops to defend the two villages to our immediate front — Clochimont and Assenois — which is only about a mile from the 101st perimeter?' He stopped and accepted the canteen cup of steaming coffee from Limey with a murmured thanks.

'Nothing's too good for the boys in the service, sir,' Limey replied cockily, wiping the spam fat from his stubbled chin with his free hand.

Hardt took a sip and handed the cup to van Fleet. 'Take a slug, Clarry,' he ordered. 'Tastes good. That English rogue must have put a shot of that Luxembourg hooch into it... Now, if Abrams appeared to be making his main effort on the Neufchâteau-Bastogne highway there — at Sibret, and then sideslipped to Assenois, might he not catch the Krauts off guard?'

Van Fleet shuddered violently as the Luxembourg rotgut burnt its way down his throat. 'That might well be, sir. But,' he raised his finger, 'the closer the roads get to Bastogne, the closer they run together. Okay, so even if Colonel Abrams does put in a feint at Sibret and then side-slips to Assenois, what's to stop the Krauts from switching troops from one place to the other at the double through those woods — there — on the map? At a rough guess, I'd say the two places are only a kilometre apart.'

'Of course, you're right, Clarry. But I've already thought of that one.'

'What do you mean, sir?'

'Clarry, we're in walking distance of Bastogne now. Even under these goddam conditions, a fit guy could probably make it in a couple of hours, don't you agree?'

'Agreed,' van Fleet answered, a little mystified by the course of the conversation.

'Now our whole goddam problem this day has been that the Krauts can see us coming and they can hear us coming too.'

Again van Fleet nodded his agreement.

'So let us assume that Clochimont is fairly strongly held by the enemy — and the same probably goes for Sibret too because it's directly in the path of Colonel Abrams — won't that mean that Assenois is only lightly held?' He hurried on before van Fleet could interrupt him. 'If that's the case, what about *two* feint attacks? The first on Clochimont, then a quick switch of roads and a second feint attack on Sibret. When Abrams has got the Krauts well and truly confused, he could put in his real and main attack at Assenois.'

'Okay, okay, skipper,' van Fleet protested. 'But in the end effect, the three villages are so close together and the country is so well-wooded, they could switch their troops to any one of the three — just like that!' He snapped his fingers together almost angrily.

Hardt looked at him with almost infuriating calm. 'I know. But what if a body of Americans were already in full occupation of Assenois when the Krauts started to switch troops? That might balance things up a bit, eh?'

Van Fleet looked at Hardt's worn, unshaven face in utter disbelief.

'You don't mean —'

'I do,' Hardt beat him to it, pleased with the effect of his surprise. '*T-Force!*'

The fires had been doused now. Soon it would be dark and too dangerous to let them continue burning; but in the still flickering embers, the watching men's faces were hollowed out to frightening death-heads so that they looked more dead than alive. Carefully Hardt straightened up and tossed away the stick with which he had drawn the rough sketch map in the snow at their feet. 'Okay, fellers, now this is the spiel. As soon as it is completely dark, we move out of here in two columns. Lieutenant van Fleet will take one, I'll take the other. We'll swing to east and west of Clochimont — here — and head north for Assenois. ETA approximately zero three hundred hours on the morning of the twenty sixth.' He waited for any reaction, but when he didn't get one, he continued hastily. 'Now some of you are probably asking yourselves, how the hell are we gonna get away with it? Both places are defended.' Hardt answered his own question. 'All day long, they've either seen us or heard us coming. This time it's different —'

'So now it's dark, Major and they won't see us!' Big Red exclaimed heartily.

'Right.'

'Yer,' Limey protested, always quicker off the mark than the rest of T-Force, 'but it's a quid to a tanner, sir, that they'll *hear* us coming all right. Old Baldy alone is rattling as if it's ripe for the knacker's yard. Together the lot of us make a heck of a racket — and it's even worse at this time of night. Noise carries a long way, a ruddy long way, after dark,' he added, his smart skinny face full of sudden foreboding.

Hardt smiled at the little Cockney. 'You'd be one hundred per cent right, Limey, if we were going to use vehicles. But we're not.'

Limey's mouth dropped open stupidly. 'Kiss me quick, me mother's drunk!' he gasped. 'Yer don't mean we're gonna use shanks' pony — in this sodding weather, Major, do you?'

'I do, Limey, I do indeed,' Major Hardt assured him. 'Tonight T-Force marches on Assenois, takes it by a *coup de main*' — there was sudden resolution in his voice — '*and holds it...*'

CHAPTER 3

General von Manteuffel was eating a Christmas dinner of captured American K-rations, standing up in the freezing great hall of his château HQ, when his phone call to the Führer came through. Hitler, far away in Franconia, wished him 'Merry Christmas'. But von Manteuffel did not return the greeting. He had other things on his mind; he got down to business at once. *'Mein Führer,'* he barked still holding the hot ration can in his free hand, 'my 2nd Panzer and Panzer Lehr have both been stopped on the Meuse. I request immediate permission to abandon the drive for Brussels.'

The hard-faced little General heard Hitler give a gasp at the other end of the line, but he went on relentlessly, knowing at the same time that he was risking his head by doing so; he wouldn't be the first German general that Hitler had sent to his death this year. 'If you give me your permission I will wheel north on this side of the Meuse and trap all Allied troops east of the river. It will be a great victory — and I shall be able to deal with that running sore of Bastogne at my leisure.' He stopped and waited for Hitler's reaction.

Surprisingly enough the Führer did not indulge himself in one of his notorious outbursts of rages with which he usually greeted any suggestion which went contrary to his wishes. Instead he said softly, almost gently. 'Not so hasty, my dear General. We have had unexpected setbacks in the Ardennes — because my original plan was not followed to the letter. But all is not lost yet. Not at all.'

Manteuffel took the opportunity to swallow a spoonful of hash and waited, his thin keen face set in a look of cynicism.

What particular white rabbit was Hitler going to pull out of the hat now?

'I see now, Manteuffel, that the Western Allies cannot be wiped out by one single dramatic blow. Good, therefore we shall envelop them in a bloody battle of attrition which will cost Churchill and Roosevelt so many men that they will beg for peace — beg for it on their knees, believe you me!'

'*Jawohl, mein Führer*' von Manteuffel muttered, unimpressed, and took another spoonful of the captured hash, wondering idly why the German Army had never been able to produce such good canned food for its soldiers.

Hitler's voice rose. 'I am sending you three new divisions, Manteuffel, and 25,000 replacements —'

The General put down the can suddenly.

'Furthermore, I am planning a new surprise for the enemy — *Northwind*, I am going to attack in Alsace to the south with new forces. That will compel that cowboy Patton to withdraw the mass of his forces now attempting to relieve Bastogne.'

This time it was von Manteuffel who gasped. The Führer was certainly producing plenty of rabbits from his hat after all.

Hitler chuckled. 'I sense you are a little surprised, my dear General. But I told you all is not lost. You will still cross the Meuse and take Brussels as planned, if you and Dietrich together wipe out the mass of the enemy troops east of the Meuse between Liège and Dinant and' — there was a sudden note of warning in Hitler's voice — 'if you capture Bastogne. I must have Bastogne — at once! It is the key to our drive for the river. And remember, Manteuffel, soon a great new German army will be taking Patton to the rear. Manteuffel, give me Bastogne and I promise you that you will be celebrating New Year in Brussels. Good night! And good luck!'

The little General put down the phone in a daze. 'Where in heaven's name was Hitler going to get the new division from?' he asked himself. But then, Hitler had done it time and time again in the past. Why couldn't he do it now? Suddenly von Manteuffel's face hardened with new resolve. He swept the ration can from the table with an impatient gesture and glared down at the map of Bastogne which lay upon it, as his suddenly alert staff officers grouped themselves around him expectantly. '*Meine Herren*,' he began, 'tomorrow we take Bastogne.' Then he started to snap out his new orders for the final attack…

Far away in the big gloomy dining-room of the Hotel Alpha, General Patton and his staff had just finished their Christmas dinner too: spam and tuna sandwiches and coffee. Now the General positioned himself in front of the meagre Christmas tree in the centre of the room and looked at his staff, the expression on his face a mixture of good humour and contempt. Most of the men present were a good twenty years younger than himself; but all of them looked much more worn and tired. The last nine days were beginning to take their toll — rapidly.

He squinted along the length of his big cigar, puffed hard, took it out of his thin cruel mouth with a flourish and started. 'Gentlemen, you look pooped and depressed. You are letting this battle get you down. You forget that battle is the most magnificent competition in which the human being can indulge. You think the Krauts are supermen. They aren't! We've licked 'em before and we'll lick them this time too!'

He paused and let his words sink in, enjoying the sudden embarrassment on their faces a little. Soon they would become angry and that would be good. On the morrow they would take out their anger on the enemy.

'We Americans are a competitive race,' he continued. 'We bet on anything — everything. We love to win. Now tomorrow we enter again in the greatest sporting event of all — battle. And we're gonna win it. How?' He answered his own question. 'By attacking the enemy and keep on attacking him. Out there in the damned foxholes, freezing their balls off tonight, no doubt, there are men who are going to die tomorrow. And do you know why they are going to die? I'll tell you. Because we are not kicking them hard enough up the ass and keeping them moving! Death in battle is a function of time and effective hostile fire. You reduce that hostile fire by your own fire — and you reduce that time element by rapid movement.' His voice descended to a hiss. Suddenly the General's cold blue eyes were empty of every emotion but naked menace. 'Tomorrow all of you are gonna get out there and root hog! I don't want any more of this goddam business of worrying about the flanks. Some darn fool once said that flanks must be secured and ever since then sons of bitches all over the world have been going crazy guarding their flanks. We're not doing that anymore in the Third Army. Let the Krauts worry about *their* flanks. Also I don't want any messages saying: "I'm holding my position." We're not holding anything, except our peckers —'

Somebody laughed, but the laughter froze on his lips as the General turned his icy gaze upon the unfortunate officer.

'Let the Hun do the holding. We shall be advancing constantly and are not interested in anything, except the enemy. We're gonna hold on to him and kick the hell outa him!'

'Tomorrow our basic plan of operation will be to advance and keep on advancing regardless of whether we have to go *over*, *under*, or *through* the enemy. Today you let me down.' He pointed the big cigar at them accusingly, noting the angry flushes which were beginning to spread over their faces. 'I promised General Eisenhower Bastogne for Christmas, and I couldn't keep that promise. George S. Patton Junior hates not being able to keep his promises. But tomorrow you are not going to let me down, because I'm not gonna let you. *Tomorrow you're gonna get Bastogne!*'

Patton broke out into his broadcast smile, though his eyes still remained cold and menacing. 'Now let me wish you Happy Christmas, good night — and sweet dreams.'

With that he swept out to the accompaniment of a few half-hearted angry 'good nights'.

Ten minutes later General Patton had dismissed his black soldier servant and was on his knees at the end of his bed, saying his nightly prayers. 'And lord,' he ended, with none of his former bravado in his voice, 'I beseech thee to give me Bastogne tomorrow... *Please Lord!*' At that particular moment, in the flickering light of the sole candle, the Commander of the half a million strong Third Army looked like a very old feeble man...

CHAPTER 4

A frozen twig cracked underfoot.

'Watch your damn foot!' Big Red hissed angrily.

'Sorry, Sarge,' Dutchie answered in a whisper.

Hardt stepped cautiously out of the snow-heavy bushes. They had circled Clochimont without incident two hours earlier. Now all that barred their progress to the village of Assenois, outlined a stark, harsh black in the icy moonlight a mile off, was the stream. Gingerly he placed his left foot into the swift-running water, which hadn't frozen in spite of the freezing temperature. The cold stabbed him like a sharp knife. '*Chrr-ist, is it cold!*' he gasped through gritted teeth.

'Let me go, sir,' Red volunteered at once.

'Nix.' Hardt answered and placed his other foot in the water. The current was strong but not too strong. He'd make it all right, if his legs didn't seize up before he got to the other bank. 'Okay, here we go!' he hissed.

Big Red took the strain on the rope which was attached to Hardt's waist. 'Okay, Major, we're ready!'

His grease gun held high above his head, Major Hardt began to wade into the freezing water.

The cold was murderous. In an instant it had marched up his legs, as swiftly as the water. It reached the base of his stomach. He gasped with the shock. Desperately he staggered forward, knowing that if he stopped now, he would black out, succumb to the blessed oblivion of unconsciousness. Gasping wildly as if he were running a great race, he passed the halfway mark. Below him he could feel the water-smoothed rocks roll and slip. Madly he fought to keep his footing. Behind him Big Red, the veins standing out at his temples, his freckled face crimson, held on grimly.

Moaning and panting, his whole body growing numb at a terrible rate in that awesome cold, Hardt staggered through the shallows in one last desperate spurt and flung himself full length in the snow of the other side. How long he lay there, gasping like a pair of broken bellows, his face pressed in the snow, he did not know. But finally Big Red's anxious whisper from the other bank made him remember the urgency of their mission. With infinite weariness, his limbs trembling uncontrollably he crawled to the nearest tree and untied the rope from his waist. His fingers bent with cold and completely without feeling, he fixed the rope to the tree. The simple movement seemed to take an age, but finally he managed it and leaning back weakly against the tree, he called: 'Okay, Red … start coming…'

Minutes later Big Red and Limey were across and the rest were following, while the little Cockney forced the last of his powerful Luxembourg schnapps between the Major's blue, trembling lips. Now there was nothing between them and the enemy in Assenois.

Major Hardt's section of T-Force crouched in a snow-bound ditch and surveyed the village. Above them Assenois lay black, squat and sinister. Nothing moved and no light showed. The fortress-like village might well have been abandoned centuries ago. But Hardt knew it wasn't. On the keen pre-dawn air, he could smell the typical odour which indicated the presence of German troops.

'Yer, they can't hide that pong o' theirs, can they, sir?' Limey expressed his thoughts in a whisper. 'It allus gives them away.'

Hardt nodded his agreement and got down to business. 'Okay, fellers,' he whispered, 'this is gonna be the drill. No firing until we're well into the place. We'll take 'em by surprise and if you bump into the Krauts, you'll —'

'Use this,' Big Red growled, holding up his ham like fist, his thick knuckles thrust through the knuckleduster grip of his short bayonet which gleamed wickedly in the fading blue light of the moon.

'Get it?'

'Get it,' Triggerman snarled. 'Knuckle sandwich it is!' They started to crawl up the hill towards the silent village in a long cautious column. Five minutes later they had reached the first house; a tumbledown wood and stone structure, bounded by a low plank fence. Hardt took a deep breath and sprang over the fence. Crouched low and expecting a burst of machinegun fire to cut the darkness frighteningly at any moment, he doubled across the snowy yard to the nearest door. The rest followed, weapons tucked to their sides to prevent them rattling. Hardt nodded his head at Big Red and pointed his finger at the door.

The big NCO nodded his head slowly to acknowledge he had understood. He crouched, legs spread apart like a gunfighter in a Hollywood cowboy movie. Slowly, very slowly, Hardt pressed the iron door handle down. It creaked rustily. Hardt gritted his teeth. The noise must have been heard all over the village! But nothing happened. Gingerly he forced open the door. Red went through it at a gallop. An instant later the rest of them were piling in.

But the room was empty. It was the same with the other rooms. Curiously Hardt looked around at the little kitchen, which smelt of stale hay, unwashed bodies, sour milk and the all-pervading odour of animal manure.

'It looks as if yer right, Major,' Limey commented, already tucking away a loaf of bread and a half-eaten length of hard garlic sausage which he had found there, 'the Jerries aren't here in force.'

'Let's hope you're not wrong, Limey,' Hardt snapped. 'Okay, fellers,' he ordered, 'round the back, through the barn and into the next house. Come on!'

The next farmhouse proved to be empty — and the next. Hardt began to believe that perhaps the village was empty after all. Swiftly the cautious file of men in the shadows slipped towards the third house. Then with frightening suddenness, it happened. The sentry detached himself from the dark well of shadow cast by a big, more prosperous-looking house to the right of the street and challenged immediately. *'Wer da!'*

Hardt reacted instinctively. He smashed the bayonet knuckleduster into the man's face. The sentry's nose cracked under the brutal impact. Thick scarlet blood splashed onto the snow. But as the man fell to his knees, his screams of agony drowned by the blood filling his throat, he pressed the trigger of his rifle. The single shot shattered the pre-dawn calm like a clarion-clear trumpet call to action.

'Alert ... alert!' a frightened voice shouted to their right.

'Los ... los, die Amis sind da!' someone else shouted and suddenly German paras were pouring into the street from houses on both sides, yelling with alarm, struggling into their uniforms, slipping the safety catches off their weapons in a frenzy of frightened fumbling. With a sinking feeling Major Hardt knew he had a battle on his hands.

The black egg of a grenade wobbled through the air towards Hardt. He ducked. Just in time. It exploded with a thick crump to his rear. Hot steel fragments scythed through the air. The T-

Force men immediately behind him went down screaming with agony. Hardt fired from the hip. The wild burst caught the para who had thrown the grenade in the chest and nearly sawed him in half. He plummeted from the shattered window and hit the bloody cobbles like a sack of wet cement.

'Get into those houses!' he yelled desperately. 'Big Red — takeover! *Quick*!'

Crouched in the middle of the street, he swung from side to side spraying its breadth with his grease gun. The advancing paras went down, arms and legs flailing crazily. Behind him the T-Force men battered the doors of the houses down frantically with their rifle butts, taking murderous casualties all the time from the Germans positioned in the windows above them. The first door gave. The GIs fought to get inside and out of the deadly fire. Another caved in. The survivors clawed their way in over the bodies of their dead and dying comrades.

'Christ on a crutch, sir!' Big Red yelled urgently and swept the upper windows to his right with a wild burst, 'get under cover before the bastards plug you!'

Hardt did not hesitate. The survivors were inside now. Crouched low he doubled towards the open door while Red covered him, the slugs striking up vicious spurts of snow at his heels. He slammed through the door and hit the bullet-pocked wall at the other side. Behind him, Big Red, firing all the while, crashed it shut with his foot. 'All right, don't stand staring there at the Major like a lot of dum-dums!' he barked, his massive chest heaving with the effort, his face blackened with powder, 'get yer asses up them stairs and start firing at the Kraut bastards!'

Hastily Trigger and Dutchie pelted up the wooden stairs to the bedrooms. There was the sound of shattering glass. A moment later their MIs began to return the enemy fire.

Hardt breathed out a long sigh. 'Wow, that was a darn near thing!' he said to no one in particular.

Limey, busy refilling a magazine from the fifty-round cloth bandolier around his chest, laughed shortly. 'You can say that again, Major. I thought we was goners just then!'

Big Red smashed out the wooden blackout board with the butt of his gun and reversing it, commenced firing well-aimed single shots at the paras in the house opposite. 'What now, sir?' he asked, his voice completely under control, as if being trapped like this was an everyday occurrence.

By an effort of will, Hardt forced his hands to stop trembling. 'What now?' he echoed the NCO's words. 'Two things.' He laughed grimly and ducked automatically as a burst of heavy machinegun fire ripped through the wall to his back as easily as if it were made of paper. 'One, we can start to pray. Two, we can only hope that Lieutenant van Fleet has already heard the firing and has drawn the right conclusion.'

'And what if the Jerries out at Clochimont have drawn the same conclusion, sir?' Limey said drily, expressing Hardt's own unspoken thought.

'Then, you little Cockney rogue, you'd better start saying some pretty powerful prayers because we're gonna sure need 'em...'

CHAPTER 5

'Hold it, fellers!' Urgently Lieutenant van Fleet held up his hand.

The weary column of T-Force men crunching through the deep snow of the fir forest stopped gratefully, while the Lieutenant turned his head to the wind to hear better. On the clear dawn air, he could make out now the quick high-pitched burr of a German Spandau and the slower answering chatter of an American BAR, sounding like some dogged, angry woodpecker.

Van Fleet knew immediately what had happened. Hardt had run into trouble up ahead at Assenois. There was no time to lose. If T-Force was to take the village before the enemy brought up reinforcements from Sibret or Clochimont, he would have to act fast. Swiftly he assessed the situation and swung round to the waiting men. 'Now listen fellers,' he explained swiftly. 'Major Hardt must have gone in through the front door in his usual way and gotten his fingers trapped rather badly.' One or two of the men chuckled wearily. 'Okay, we're gonna go in through the back door. If we're lucky, we'll catch the Krauts by surprise and give them a nasty kick in the *derrière*.' He looked at their faces. They were unshaven, cold and weary, but determined. They had a lot of fight left still in them. 'Okay, fellers,' he ordered, 'let's go!'

As usual the German foxhole was so well camouflaged that they were on top of it before they knew it. Van Fleet's heart missed a beat. The German para was crouched right in front of him, blending in perfectly with the snow in his white snow jacket. For what seemed an age the two young men, American and German, stared at each other. Then the German started to raise his machine pistol. Van Fleet was quicker off the mark. He dived forward. His knife grazed off the para's rimless helmet. The German grunted with triumph. He smashed the metal butt of the Schmeisser in van Fleet's face. The American howled with pain. But he knew he must not let the man raise the alarm. Desperately he lashed out with his knife again. The sharp blade bored deep into the German's throat. There was a sound like gas escaping from a punctured main. Together they fell to the bottom of the foxhole in a confused heap. Van Fleet felt the German beginning to go limp beneath him. But he was taking no chances. He thrust in the knife again, viciously. Blood ran over his hand and wrist in a hot stream. Still the para did not die.

'For chrissake, *die*, you Kraut bastard!' he croaked desperately and plunged home the knife once more. The German's spine arched. Blood spurted out of both nostrils. His eyes turned upwards, only the whites showing. Then he was dead and the T-Force men were hauling a shaking, vomiting van Fleet out of the bloody hole.

They caught the Germans attacking the trapped T-Force men by complete surprise. What happened next was a massacre, not war. At fifty yards' range they poured a concentrated hail of fire into the unsuspecting paras' backs. The Germans went down by the score, galvanised into terrible frantic action by the lead pumping into their defenceless bodies, jerking and twitching on the snowy ground at each new blow until death overcame them. A couple of them tried to break away. Van Fleet dropped one with his forty-five. Twisting and turning frantically like a football player making an end run, another dodged the bullets. At van Fleet's side a burly corporal waited his chance. As the panic-stricken, wild-eyed para came level, he launched a tremendous kick at the man's crotch.

The German went down as if he were poleaxed, his false teeth bulging out of his vomit-filled mouth. As he lay writhing there in the snow, the corporal smashed the heel of his boot into the para's face, a look of absolute animal pleasure on his unshaven features. Once, twice, three times. Van Fleet could hear the facial bones splinter each time. He turned away with a shudder of horror. And then the heart went out of the handful of survivors. Frantically, as if the metal were burning their hands, they threw away their weapons. '*Kamerad ... Kamerad*' they cried piteously. '*Nicht schiessen!*'

But the battle-crazed T-Force men, their blood roused by the mad excitement of combat, continued to fire into the defenceless Germans until Big Red's angry voice bellowed from the closest house: 'Will you bastards stop firing! Don't ya recognise a prisoner when you see one?... Now knock it off, willya!'

Moments later van Fleet and Hardt were shaking hands as if they had been apart for a score of years. 'Boy, am I glad to see you, Clarry!' Hardt cried exuberantly. 'They certainly had us by the short and curlies just then. Thank God you made it!'

'Yeah, I've been doing a bit of praying myself over the last few minutes, skipper,' van Fleet said wearily and slumped against the wall, which was pocked by bullets as if with the symptoms of some loathsome skin disease.

Hardt took in the younger man's swollen cheek, rapidly going a deep purple. 'Take five, Clarry,' he said sympathetically, 'and get one of the medics to have a look at that mug of yours.

At the moment you've got a face that only a mother could love.'

'Yeah — and only with difficulty at that,' van Fleet answered and limped away to find a medic.

Hardt dismissed him from his mind and swung round, looking for Limey. He spotted him, bent over a dead para officer, busily engaged in stripping off the watch from a hand already stiffening in the icy cold. 'Limey,' he bellowed. 'Over here at the double!'

The little cockney pulled off the watch with one final tug and stuffing it into his pocket, ran over to the waiting officer. 'Don't you know, Limey, that's against regulations?' he snapped! 'Looting the dead'.

Limey winked at him cheekily. 'I wasn't looting, sir. Ner! That Jerry officer had left the watch to me in his will.'

Hardt shook his head. 'No wonder the British Army didn't want you.'

'I'm Monty's personal present to the American Army, sir. A weally experienced chap like that' — he gave a malicious parody of the British Field Marshal's manner of speech — 'will be wather good for you American chappies. A wipping way to learn the art of war.'

'And you'll get the wipping toe of my boot up your limey ass,' Hardt said, trying to fight back his laughter, 'if you don't get your butt in there and behind the radio! I want you to send this message to Colonel Abrams immediately!'

Limey had hardly finished at the transmitter, when from the direction of Clochimont, the German batteries opened up with a sudden, frightening roar. Hardt bit his lips anxiously. The enemy was reacting more quickly than he had anticipated. Abrams would have to move even more swiftly now, if he were going to exploit the new situation.

'*Hot dog!*' Abrams cried delightedly, as the staff captain handed him the decoded message and he could read the good news in plain text. 'I knew old Hairless Harry would come through in the end!'

Colonel Jaques, Commander of the 53rd Armoured Infantry, who was scheduled to lead the last attack on Bastogne on the following day, was not so impressed by the message from Assenois. 'I don't know so much, Creighton. If we take the Assenois route to Bastogne, we're still faced with Clochimont and by the sound of that —' he inclined his crew-cut head in the direction of the artillery fire — 'the Krauts will have a hot reception waiting for us.'

Abrams' broad grin disappeared. He knew what the infantry colonel meant. Combat Command R had only sufficient tanks and infantry left for one major push. If he selected the Assenois route and the breakthrough attempt failed, he knew from the information coming out of Bastogne, the garrison would not hold out another day. The Krauts were already within rifle shot distance of McAuliffe's CP.

Abrams pulled out a big cigar and stuck it in his mouth in conscious imitation of his idol, Patton. His face impassive now, he considered the problem. Should he attack through Sibret at dawn as was already planned, now the crater which barred their way was filled in; or should he attempt a feint at Clochimont, as Hardt's T-Force had obviously done, and then barrel on for Assenois, breaking through the thin screen of enemy infantry between the two villages — and then on to Bastogne?

Suddenly the burly tank commander was assailed by doubts. But what if his feint at Clochimont didn't succeed? What would happen too, if Hardt couldn't hold Assenois long enough? After all his T-Force were only armed with the lightest weapons and once the enemy became aware of the cuckoo's egg which had been laid in their nest, they could well throw in armour. He bit deep into the big cigar. If he made the wrong decision now, not only would he sacrifice the lives of the 10,000 airborne troops trapped in Bastogne, he would give the Krauts the key road junction which barred the path to the River Meuse.

Suddenly he made his decision. 'Okay, Jaques, it's too big for me. Let the brass make the decision.'

Together the two colonels stumbled through the snowy darkness towards Abrams command tank 'Thunderbolt IV'. 'Operator,' he barked at the sleepy radio operator, 'get me General Gaffey.'

The man looked at him with alarm in the green glowing gloom of the icy turret. 'But sir,' he protested, 'it's two o' clock in the morning!'

'I don't give a monkey's goddam,' Abrams snarled. 'You're up, I'm up. The whole goddam Combat Command is up at this Godforsaken hour. Why should the General lie in his nice soft warm bed. *Get me Gaffey!*'

General Gaffey was aghast. 'But Creighton, we've got the Sibret business worked out to the last detail! Now you want me to authorize an attack in a completely different direction. Don't you realise —'

'I do, sir,' Abrams snapped, angry at the freezing cold of the Sherman's turret, the war, the fact that he hadn't had any sleep for the last thirty-six hours. 'I realise exactly what the implications of any failure will be?'

At the other end of the line, Gaffey wiped his dry mouth. The Fourth was his first divisional command and he still felt uneasy with the élite armoured division. If he made the wrong decision now, it might mean the end of his whole career; and one didn't throw a thirty-year long career for the sake of a snap decision in the middle of the night.

'Sir, I want to go on record,' Abrams barked, irritated by the long silence, perhaps reading the General's mind too, 'that I advocated the Assenois route as the best way to break through?'

'Okay, okay, Crighton, don't ride me,' Gaffey answered, a little helplessly. 'Hell, I'm not Jesus, you know! I can't see what's gonna happen tomorrow. You don't make decisions like this in a matter of seconds?'

'Somebody's got to make a decision, sir!' Abrams persisted.

'Okay, so be it. But let the Old Man make the decision.'

'You mean, General Patton, sir?'

'Yes,'

'But sir,' Abrams protested. 'That may take hours and we just don't have that kind of time. I don't know how long Hardt's men can hold out at Assenois.'

'You've heard my decision, Abrams? Gaffey snapped with the full authority of a divisional commander behind him, now that he had passed the buck to Patton. 'You'll just have to abide with it. Good night.'

'Good night, sir,' Abrams put down the radio phone and stared blankly at the smooth turret wall, the trickles of melting ice streaming down it like cold tears. Over from the direction of Assenois, the volume of German fire was increasing by the second. *Would Hardt be able to hold till the morning?*

CHAPTER 6

Below the village the road lay awesome and brooding, and somehow expectant. Dead German paratroopers were scattered everywhere: ghastly tableaux of bodies, a frozen hand held up to the grey merciless sky, as if pleading for aid; a bloody stump, the red transformed by the cold to a harsh, hard black; eyes staring accusingly from waxen faces.

But Hardt had no eyes for the dead this new morning. His gaze was fixed on the hills beyond, searching the far distance for the first sign of Abrams' tanks, a look almost of longing in his eyes.

Beside him van Fleet, his face heavily bandaged, lowered his glasses with a sigh. 'No sign of them, skipper.' Hardt did the same. 'No,' he said miserably. 'Not a sausage. God, it looks as if the war has stopped out there and they've forgotten to inform us that it has!'

'I'm afraid you're wrong, sir,' Limey standing behind them, said quietly. 'Look over there!'

As the blood-red ball of the winter sun started to creep over the jagged black edge of the fir forest to their left, the watching men could see the first of the German cannon being pushed out of the trees into the open.

'The buggers are bloody confident that we can't hit them at that range, aren't they, sir?' Limey said bitterly.

Hardt nodded his head slowly. 'Yes, they're confident all right.' He cupped his hands around his mouth. 'Okay, everywhere, you'd better take cover now,' he shouted. 'You can expect incoming mail in about — five minutes flat!' Major Hardt was one minute out. At precisely 8.25 on the morning of

December 26th, 1944, the German artillery opened up. With a mighty antiphonal crash, the first salvo burst on the village.

Everywhere purple tongues of flame leapt up from the rooftops. The ancient farm buildings collapsed like houses made of cards. A farm cart, filled with turnips for the cattle, flew high in the air. Turnips smacked into the walls and splattered there like smashed heads. A couple of plough horses broke out of their stable. Manes and tails blazing a fiery red, brown eyes wild with terror, they clattered down the street like something out of an ancient Nordic saga.

The merciless shelling seemed to have no pattern. It was aimless and incessant. Yet as Hardt cowered at the bottom of the foxhole behind a shattered, burning farmhouse, he knew there was method behind the German barrage. The enemy wanted to keep them pinned down to give their infantry a chance to get in close enough. As the earth shook and shuddered, he forced himself to raise his head and cry at the men, cowering together in abject misery all around him. 'Get ready, men … it won't be long before they start to put in their foot soldiers!'

Big Red, bleeding from the nose and ears, added his voice to the Major's. 'Yeah, when them Krauts start coming up the hill, I want you joes waiting for them — or else!' He ducked hastily as a fresh salvo of shells swamped the houses.

And then as suddenly as it had started, the barrage ended, leaving behind it a loud echoing silence, heavy with menace. Awed, white-eyed with shock, banging their ears with the palms of their hands to clear away the ringing noises, the T-Force men took up their firing positions and waited…

'Well, General?' Abrams demanded with scant respect.

Ahead of 'Thunderbolt IV', a Sherman was burning fiercely, enshrouded in thick white smoke, and automatically Abrams told himself that it was no wonder tankers called the Sherman 'ronson'; it went up in flames as soon as a shell came within sniffing distance of its goddam gasoline engine.

'Nothing,' Gaffey replied at the other end of the line.

'What do you mean — *nothing*?' Abrams exploded, forgetting the rank now in his anger.

'Put a "sir" on that, Abrams,' Gaffey snapped. 'You heard me — nothing. I've been in touch with Army HQ, but General Patton doesn't seem to have reported in yet.'

'Jesus Christ, *sir*, you don't know what it's like up here, *sir*. The Heinies are throwing everything but the goddam kitchen sink at us — and I expect that at any moment.' He ran his eye along the road ahead, lined with burning Shermans and what looked like bundles of rags abandoned in the snow. 'From where I am now, *sir*, I can count four of our tanks knocked out — and a good couple of dozen dead doughs. I've got to have that decision now, *sir*!... I haven't gotten more than a couple of hours left.'

'I can't help that, Abrams. As I told you this morning, I'm going to let the Old Man make the decision. Until we hear to the contrary from him, you will simply have to stick to the original plan. *Got it*?' Gaffey barked with an air of finality.

'Got it, *sir*,' Abrams said miserably and put down the radio phone.

He dropped off the Sherman's deck and took in the scene ahead. It was now nearly midday. At one o'clock, he was due to kick off the attack, direction Sibret. But already he was down to twenty tanks, only enough for one good assault. The barrel was scraped clean; after they were gone, he was finished. What was he going to do?

In Bastogne the end was near now. On all sides, Manteuffel's new divisions and the reinforcements Hitler had sent him were pressing home their attack with unrelenting fury.

Elite SS troopers from the premier SS Division — the Bodyguard; veterans of the Desert, Russia and Normandy from the 15th Panzer; Hitler's own personal troops from the Führer Escort Brigade; keen, young ex-Hitler Youth fanatics from the People's Grenadier Divisions: on that day the élite of the German Army was attempting to carry out the Fifth Army Commander's harsh order: '*Today we wipe Bastogne off the map!*'

At the 101st red brick CP, sweating, frustrated staff officers ran back and forth with ever more alarming reports from the front — 'C Company is being overrun ... K is down to one officer now ... tanks directly below my window ... am bugging out fast ... we're firing at the bastards at point-blank range ... but they're still coming in their hundreds...'

And time and time again, the waiting cooks, clerks, lightly wounded and drivers formed in a last ditch reserve to defend the CP against the enemy when they came — which would be soon — looked longingly to the south. But the white covered hills there were bare of anything save Germans, ever more Germans. There was no sign of the relief column. It looked as if the 'battered bastards of Bastogne', as they were now calling themselves with cynical fatalism, had been abandoned to their fate.

The whole valley below Assenois quaked. From one end of the German positions to the other, the angry red lights blinked like enormous furnaces. The hills boomed to the tremendous roar. With a hoarse scream, more than two hundred shells ripped through the grey sky above the heads of the advancing infantry and smacked into Assenois. In a flash it had disappeared in a choking yellow fog of acrid explosive smoke. The German infantry broke into an awkward run.

The T-Force men huddled in their cellars and foxholes, as the whole hillside shook and swayed like a ship which had just run into a violent storm. Holes collapsed. Hysterically screaming, the wounded fought the soil, clawing their way out with hands that ran with blood. A cellar was hit. In an instant it became a red, gory mess, pieces of bodies and limbs plastered to the shattered walls like postage stamps.

A GI broke under the strain. He sprang from his hole. Before anyone could stop him, he was pelting clumsily down the debris-littered burning street, waving his helmet at the advancing Germans, as if he were a schoolboy welcoming a parade. But he didn't get far. A shell landed fifty yards away. It ripped off both his legs, and suddenly he was stumbling forward on his bloody stumps reduced to the size of a child until he could continue no more. As the bombardment ceased and the infantry charged, he dropped on his face in the snow.

'On yer feet everybody!' Red yelled urgently.

Hardt blew his whistle. 'Standfast,' he cried desperately. '*Fire at will!*'

A stick grenade sailed through the air and exploded to his right. Something slapped against his helmet. It set his head off ringing. Abruptly it began to ache like hell. But he had no time to worry about the pain. The enemy was almost upon them.

He ran to a heap of smoking debris, grease gun at the ready. A dirty face under a rimless helmet loomed out of the smoke. He fired instinctively. The para dropped heavily. Another man came at him from the right. He was unarmed. But Hardt knew there was no time to worry about that now. He pressed the trigger of his grease gun. Nothing happened! He had a stoppage. A second later the German was on him. Hardt dropped his grease gun and grappled with the man. But the man wouldn't let go. Hardt thrust his two forefingers into his nostrils and tugged. The para screamed. Blood streamed down Hardt's hands. Yet still the German hung on, his hands pressed into the flesh of the Major's throat now. Frantic with fear, knowing that at any moment, one of the German's comrades might thrust his bayonet into his exposed back, and gasping for air, he squirmed and struggled wildly, trying to free himself before he blacked out.

'Let go of the Major, will yer, you Jerry sod!' the familiar English voice cried angrily.

It was Limey. Next moment, he brought the brassbound butt of his rifle down on the back of the para's neck. He pitched to the ground wordlessly. Limey didn't hesitate. Placing his muddy boot on the man's twitching body, he crashed his butt into the side of the para's face. There was a sound like thin ice cracking underfoot Black blood started to pour from the dying man's ears.

Now the paras were everywhere. All along the ragged line held by T-Force there were cursing, screaming gasping men swaying back and forth in individual combat. Hardt pushed his way through them, followed by Limey, and threw himself down behind an abandoned 50 calibre. Just in time! The second wave of infantry were scrambling up the hill, yelling in triumph. With Limey covering him, Hardt pressed the trigger.

At that range he couldn't miss. They went down by the score. But Hardt didn't take his finger off the trigger. Now he, too, was overcome by a blood rage. None of them would escape. Swinging the dull glowing gun from right to left, he hosed them down expertly. Frantically the survivors broke and ran for cover. They never reached it. Their backs riddled with lead, they dropped twitching and quaking to die among their already fallen comrades.

Behind him T-Force had finished off the first wave. But there was no time to rest. A third wave of paras had emerged from the trees and, urged on by bareheaded young officers who waved their machine pistols in encouragement, they were stumbling up the body littered slope. Gasping asthmatically like old men, their limbs trembling uncontrollably, the T-Force men took aim.

Hardt's 50 calibre chattered into violent life. Tracer swept the air. It acted as a signal for the rest. Firing broke out everywhere. Still the Germans came on, their numbers getting ever fewer by the instant.

'Concentrate on the officers!' Big Red cried.

Trigger needed no urging. Springing up from his foxhole, his mouth slack and wet, filled with terrible obscenities, he took aim as if he were back on the range at Fort Bliss. Officer after officer pitched to the ground, shot through the head. Still the Germans kept on coming.

Then abruptly when it seemed they would swamp the American positions, they broke. In an instant, they were streaming down the hillside in panic, tugging and clawing at each other, tossing away their weapons as they ran.

'Gor blimey,' Limey yelled enthusiastically, 'get a gander at that, Major! It's better than the sodding Derby!'

But there was no answering light in Major Hardt's eyes. For as the crackle of small arms fire started to die away everywhere and the cries of the fleeing paras grew even fainter, he could hear another sound coming from the woods to their right: the rusty clatter of metal tracks and the grind of powerful diesel engines ascending the steep heights. His heart sank. The Krauts were bringing up tanks.

CHAPTER 7

It was now one thirty.

Abrams and Jaques stood shivering in the icy air, watching their tanks and infantry getting ready for the final assault on Sibret. There was still no message from Gaffey, yet as Abrams surveyed a silent Sibret he knew instinctively that the village was well defended.

'Penny for your thoughts, Creighton,' Jaques broke the uneasy silence.

'At this moment, they aren't worth a plug —' Abrams broke off suddenly and swung round. A great roar was filling the air from the west. Like fat silver geese, swarms of C-47s began to come across the Fourth's positions. Over Bastogne the German flak opened up. Still they came on. Hundreds of bright parachutes sprang open, filling the sky like a field of sudden poppies. Now the gliders were released and started to hush down through the brown puffballs of exploding shells. One was hit and went straight down in a nose-dive, spilling tiny, wildly flailing figures out of its side, which were men. Another was destroyed in mid-air, disappearing in a vicious spurt of scarlet flame. And another!

The brave sight made Abrams mind up for him. 'If they can do it, so can we!' he cried abruptly.

'Do what?'

'Stick out our necks like those flyboys up there, instead of sitting on our fat keesters here, just waiting for orders.'

Jaques looked at Abrams, his big cigar stuck out like a tank 75mm. 'What are you going to do, Creighton?' he asked, knowing the Tank Colonel's hot temper.

'I'll tell you what I'm goddamwell gonna do — I'm gonna call Patton myself and ask him for permission to take Assenois.'

'Jesus, Creighton,' Jaques protested aghast, 'you can't do that! Bird colonels just don't call army commanders for orders. You've got to go through channels. You're a Pointer like me. You goddam well ought to know that...'

But his mind made up, Abrams was already running to 'Thunderbolt IV' to carry out his plan.

It took over an hour to reach General Patton with Abrams' harassed, sweating radio operator pleading, threatening, cajoling his way up the net until he was finally connected with Third Army HQ. For a moment Abrams felt a sense of fear when the operator handed him the telephone, hand over the mouthpiece, and whispered, 'It's the General himself, sir!' He knew he wouldn't be the first field grade officer that Old Blood and Guts had busted right down to private, West Point or no West Point. Then he flung all hesitation to the winds. 'Gimme the damned thing!' he snarled and plucked the phone out of the pale-faced operator's sweating hand.

'General, this is Abrams — Creighton Abrams!'

If Patton were surprised, he did not show it. His somewhat high-pitched voice did not change in any way, as he said: 'And what can I do for you, Creighton?'

'General, will you authorize a big risk with Combat Command R for a breakthrough to Bastogne?'

'What is it?'

Swiftly Colonel Abrams explained his new plan. It was greeted by a silence, which seemed to last for an age. Finally when Abrams was already beginning to see himself stripped down to the rank of private, totting a rifle in some infantry company or other, Patton said with sudden enthusiasm: 'I sure as hell will authorize that risk! And Creighton?'

'Sir?'

'Never call your army commander *direct* again, son.' Patton chuckled throatily. 'The brass don't like it. It disturbs their ivory tower calm.'

'Will do, sir?'

A second later, Abrams was running frantically towards the waiting tankers like an excited schoolboy released from school at the end of a long boring day, crying: 'It's the push, fellers!'

Swiftly Abrams outlined his plan to Captain Dwight who would be in charge of the column, and Lieutenant Boggess, one of his veterans from France who would be at point with his nine forty-ton Cobra Kings, the Division's largest tanks. With his eyes glinting, rolling his big cigar from one side of his mouth to the other, he ended with the words, 'We're going in to those people now. Let 'er roll!'

Swiftly the column of tanks, armoured cars and half-tracks, filled with infantry, got underway, rattling through a patch of snowy woods and then up the steep hill which led to Assenois. Abrams, in the middle of the column, was glued to his radio, waiting for the first indication from Boggess that he had run into trouble. The call for help came exactly at four o'clock. Boggess had spotted German armour and dug-in antitank guns waiting for him at the outskirts of the besieged village. Abrams pressed the mike button, which linked him with four whole artillery battalions. 'Concentration Number Nine,' he barked excitedly, 'and play it soft and sweet.' Then he slumped back against the cold wall of 'Thunderbolt IV', abruptly drained of all energy. He had done all he could. Now it was out of his hands. Now everything depended upon Boggess.

The artillery had done their work well. The whole slope outside of the village was littered with burning, destroyed German tanks and antitank guns. One solitary antitank opposed him as he lined for the last dash. It managed to get off a wild shell, which whizzed by the column harmlessly. The next moment the German gunners were running for their lives, pursued by the concentrated fire of nine tank machineguns. 'Okay, fellers, here we go!' Boggess yelled over the intercom. '*Now!*' The nine Cobra Kings rattled forward in line, firing to left and right. Now the outskirts of the village were as dark as night, the winter sun shut out by the smoke and dust. Two tanks took the wrong turn and disappeared into a side street. A half-track was hit by one of their own shells and crashed to a stop, blocking the progress of the rest of the column. Swiftly the Germans took advantage of the forced halt. The paras swarmed out of their positions. In the smoke and confusion a wild mêlée broke out. Men were locked out together in hand to hand combat, stabbing, slashing, shooting each other mercilessly.

Armoured infantry jumped off the other half-tracks. A redheaded 19-year old charged a German gun position in the smoke. 'Come on out!' he screamed, almost hysterically. A German poked his head up from a foxhole. The Private shot him in the neck. He ran to the next hole, bashing in the head of a terrified German with the butt of his rifle. Still screaming the redhead disappeared into the smoke.

Behind him, lying wounded in both legs, his company commander tried to sort out the confused mess. But Boggess had no time to lose. He couldn't wait any longer for the infantry follow-up. Alone, save two other Cobra Kings, he barrelled through the northern end of the village. Men in familiar uniforms rose up from the shattered ruins on both sides and waved frantically. Boggess waved back: they had to be the survivors of Hardt's T-Force. But he wasn't stopping to discuss the situation. He had to get to Bastogne before dark — *he had to!*

'After the sodding Lord Mayor's show — the dust carts!' Limey exclaimed with disgust, as Boggess and his tanks disappeared and were followed by a group of German paras being slowly pressed backwards through the village by the armoured infantrymen. With a sigh he dropped down next to Hardt and took aim once again.

Boggess was now moving very fast. The King Cobra swayed from side to side on the high-crowned road and Boggess prayed the tank wouldn't lose a track; then he would be sunk. Behind him the remaining three tanks of his company were beginning to catch up. But there was still a three hundred yard gap between the two groups of King Cobras. Two Germans ran out of the firs after the first three tanks had passed and dropped a couple of teller mines on the road before doubling madly back into their cover. In the ever growing gloom the driver of the scout half-track leading the tanks did not see the mines, until it was too late. He braked hard and slid directly over the tellers. They exploded with a tremendous roar, heaving the six ton half-track right in the air. When it came down, both its tracks were gone and its hood was flipped open like the lid of a can of sardines. The second group of tanks came to an abrupt halt behind the wrecked vehicle.

Boggess cursed. But still he was not going to stop. He was nearly there now. But the light was going fast. The three remaining tanks would soon be easy meat for any enemy bazooka man lurking in the gloomy, snow-heavy firs. 'Keep that gun going,' he ordered his bow machine gunner. 'Or they'll slip it to us — hard, Kafner.'

Kafner needed no warning. He was well aware of the danger. As they came ever closer to their objective, he sprayed the firs on both sides of the road with bullet after bullet until the barrel of his machinegun began to glow a dull angry red.

The minutes passed. In the gloomy buttoned-down turret, Boggess watched the dim figures of both sides run and fall. The woods seemed full of Germans. But the Cobra Kings' attack had come too suddenly for the enemy to react with their deadly bazookas. They rattled through safely. Then it was abruptly lighter. They were in open country again. There were a few bushes with coloured parachutes draped upon them, but that was all. A concrete blockhouse loomed up to his right. It looked empty, but Boggess wasn't taking any chances. 'Give it a couple of rounds,' he ordered Dickerson, his 75mm gunner. The gunner responded immediately. The turret swung round, and he was on target in a flash. The 75mm cracked into action. The tank shuddered — once, twice, three times. Empty rounds clattered to the deck. Ahead great chunks of concrete flew off the pillbox; but there was no answering fire. The place was obviously empty after all.

'Cease firing!' Boggess yelled urgently.

Both Dickerson and Kafner took their fingers off their triggers.

'What is it, sir?' someone asked.

'I don't know,' Boggess answered slowly, squinting through the periscope, 'but I think ... I think they might be our guys.'

'Hot shit!' Dickerson yelled.

'Slow down driver,' Boggess commanded and making a decision, raised the turret cover. To his front, men in what looked like American uniform were crouched in foxholes on both sides of the road.

Cupping his hands around his mouth Boggess yelled: 'Come on out!'

The men in the holes stayed stubbornly where they were, their hands on their weapons. They made no response.

'It's all right,' Boggess called. 'It's the Fourth Armoured Division.'

Still the men in the holes would not move. Dickerson and Kafner crawled on to the turret and added their voices to that of their commander. Several helmeted heads rose suspiciously slowly from the foxholes. Finally a man crawled from the ground and came cautiously towards the waiting tanks, his carbine levelled on the men on the turret; there had been too much talk about Krauts wearing American uniforms these last few days. He was taking no chances.

'I'm Lieutenant Webster of the 101st Airborne,' he said solemnly and unsmilingly.

Boggess grinned broadly, shoving back his leather tanker's helmet. 'Glad to meet you, Lieutenant. My name's Boggess of the Fourth Armoured. Bastogne has just been relieved!'

The Airborne Lieutenant nodded absently, as if Boggess had just remarked on the state of the weather. 'Have you got any water?' he asked quite unemotionally, 'we ain't had a drink all goddam day.'

CHAPTER 8

Sirens shrieking crazily, the two motorcycle outriders hissed over the brow of the hill, zig-zagging between the smouldering debris of war and skidded to a halt in front of Major Hardt. A moment later the scout car followed more cautiously, its deck bristling with 50 calibre machineguns, its tall antenna whipping in the icy wind, the General's bodyguards scowling suspiciously at the bodies of dead paratroopers sprawled everywhere, fingers around the triggers of their tommy guns.

Standing upright in his jeep, as if he were some Roman emperor in a chariot, wearing his 'war face', his pugnacious jaw jutting against the webbing strap of his glistening, lacquered helmet with its enormous three stars, General Patton took in the scene as they drove slowly into Assenois. The German tanks burned black against the hills like great dead animals in the snow. The snow-covered mounds, once men, which dotted the landscape. A human leg, complete with German jackboot, dangling from a shell-stripped tree like a piece of monstrous human fruit.

Then he had seen enough. Imperiously he held up his hand. Sergeant Mims applied the brakes and the jeep came to a stop in front of the tired, dirty, survivors of T-Force.

Hardt managed a weary salute. Patton, aware that the newsreel cameras were already whirring, returned the salute with the zest of a captain of cadets at West Point at the passing out parade. 'No picnic, eh, Hardt?' he snorted and indicated the shattered scenery of war with the swagger stick he always carried on such publicity exercises.

'No, sir. It wasn't,' Hardt agreed, blinking a little in the glare from the Signal Corps photographers' flashes.

'Well done all the same, Hardt — and well done all you men, too,' he added, raising his voice so that the survivors could hear him. 'You fellers certainly saved the 101st's bacon for them.' He stuck out his gloved hand. 'Put it there, Hardt!'

Utterly exhausted, Hardt took the General's hand, while Patton posed obligingly for the photographers. 'Okay, fellers, that's enough. We've got to get on to Bastogne now. We're holding up the parade, you know.' Releasing Hardt's hand he pointed to the great column of vehicles — tanks, trucks, half-tracks, ambulances — heading for Bastogne. He beamed suddenly at Hardt. 'And you son, get in my jeep with me.'

'With you sir?'

'Yeah, you made it possible for my armour to break through to Bastogne, the least you deserve is a chance of being able to see the place.'

'But my men —' Hardt began to protest.

Patton steered him gently to the jeep. 'Don't worry about them — I'm having an extra Christmas dinner brought up for them. Turkey and all the trimmings — and there'll be a bottle of beer for each man too.'

'Did you hear that?' Limey exploded when the howl of the sirens had died away and Patton had disappeared to be followed by the great convoy, heading for Bastogne. '*A bottle of beer for each man*! Cor ferk a duck, yer'd think he was giving us the ruddy crown jewels!'

Dutchie wiped a dirty hand across his unshaven face and took his eyes off the passing trucks. 'Yeah, you could be right there. But I could go that bottle of beer all the same.'

'Yer not the only one neither, Dutchie. But yer gonna have a bloody long wait here till yer get it, mate.'

The little Englishman nodded at the supply trucks passing in a seemingly never-ending stream. 'Yer can guess who's gonna get the first priority this day can't you? Beer, grub, the lot — it'll all be going up to the Airborne, believe you me. With all that brass up there and them newspapermen as well, it stands to reason.' He broke off suddenly, a cunning look in his red-rimmed tired eyes. 'You're a religious bloke, aren't you?' he asked. Dutchie looked at him stupidly. 'I guess so.'

'Well, you'll probably know that bit in the Bible where it says "if the beer won't come to Jesus, then Jesus must go to the beer"?'

'Can't say I ever heard of that one, Limey,' Dutchie said slowly. The Englishman nudged him swiftly. 'Silly bugger, I was only pulling yer leg. But if they won't send us any beer, then we've got to go and find it ourselves.'

'You mean Bastogne?'

'*Natch*!'

More and more trucks and jeeps, pulling little trailers loaded high with cannon shells, bumped over the frozen, shell-pitted road past the two waiting T-Force men. The column halted for a moment and Limey called up to the big black soldier behind the wheel: 'Whatcher mate, got a bit of room till Bastogne?' The man shook his head. 'No deal, soldier.' He jerked a lazy thumb at the back of the truck. 'Just filled right up — sorr-ee!' As the truck started to move again, Dutchie said: 'Hey, look Limey, he's got a couple of goddam civvies in the back. That sguy was kidding us.'

Limey caught a glimpse of two ragged civilians who were somehow familiar — he didn't know from where — and shrugged. 'Racial prejudice, I 'spect,' he commented and raised his thumb hopefully, once more.

At the back of the truck, Steiner breathed out a sigh of relief, but said nothing. He didn't need to. Todt knew that the two white soldiers rapidly fading away behind them might have started asking awkward questions. Their cover as two Belgian civilians intent on going back to their homes in Bastogne, which so easily satisfied the soft-hearted black soldier, would perhaps not have stood up to their questions. He winked at the pinched-face frozen Major. Solemnly Steiner winked back.

Now they were getting even closer to Bastogne and their target. The death and destruction of the recent fighting stretched to the very horizon. Shattered trucks, burnt and grotesquely contorted tanks, unrecognisable blackened, tangled heaps of wreckage — and everywhere the upended rifles sticking out of the mounds of snow like a denuded forest which indicated that a man lay dead beneath.

A column of German prisoners shambled by the convoy going the other way. Feet wrapped in sacking, women's shawls and blankets wrapped round their heads, louse-ridden and freezing, they plodded westwards, leaving the red-flecked, yellow trail of dysentery in their wake. Steiner bit his lip. His countrymen in defeat did not look so good; their will had been broken completely.

The long convoy began to rumble into Bastogne itself. Through the shattered window of one of the first houses, Steiner caught a glimpse of a bearded American paratrooper lighting a fire beneath the frozen body of a German soldier hanging by a rope from the beams. 'His boots,' Todt commented laconically. 'He wants his boots!'

Steiner's revulsion was mingled with bitter contempt and hate. As the convoy started to slow down prior to stopping, he whispered, 'Todt, after that business at the bridge, I was tempted to say that we should give up. We had done enough. But that just now,' Steiner's eyes flashed with their old angry determination, 'that just now had made me realise that we've got to make them pay for Bastogne, even if it costs our own lives.'

'And so the heroes of Bastogne have a new watchword,' the portly, bespectacled Colonel completed the citation, his breath fogging the crisp air. 'It belongs in the bright lexicon of the fighting man along with "Don't Give Up the Ship!... Don't Shoot Till You See the Whites of Their Eyes" and "Send More Japanese".' He raised his head and beamed benignly at a waiting Patton. 'From this time onwards "Nuts" will forever symbolize American courage under fire.'

'Balls!' Patton grunted irreverently under his breath to Hardt. 'The silly bastards should not have gotten themselves surrounded in the first place!'

But as the cameras commenced whirring once more, he stepped forward to meet McAuliffe with no trace of his irritation on his lean face. 'Well, McAuliffe,' he said, pinning on the DSC he had awarded the Airborne Commander, 'I guess you and your boys are heroes, eh?'

'Who, us sir?'

'Sure.' Patton fumbled with the decoration's pin. 'Everybody was worried about you.'

'Hell, sir,' McAuliffe said pugnaciously. 'My Geronimo are ready to attack any time you want them to!'

'Well spoken, McAuliffe.'

'Y-a-a-ay!' a ragged cheer went up from the watching paratroopers and an utterly weary Hardt, who was having difficulty in keeping his eyes open in spite of the icy wind, couldn't help thinking that the Airborne men looked in better shape than his own battered T-Force back in Assenois.

Patton pressed McAuliffe's hand, beaming boisterously. 'Congratulations, General, you got your medal. Now if you'll give me five minutes to have a pee — when you get to my age it don't go so quick — and then we'll go out in the field and have a look at some of those sky boys of yours.'

'Now there's a soldier who loves his weapon like his mother,' Steiner said thoughtfully, as the crowds started to drift away to reveal the bare-headed young soldier squatting in the doorway of a ruined house, caressing the automatic rifle carefully, almost lovingly, applying a light film of oil along its black gleaming length.

Todt grunted noncommittally. He had seen soldiers like that before, who had fallen in love with their weapons, and were completely intrigued by the functional efficiency of the wheels, the triggers, the telescopic sights.

'I bet a soldier like that is saddened that he has to leave it outside at night. You can see it. For him it's like having to abandon a pet dog in the elements. That soldier loves his rifle.'

Todt grinned suddenly. 'You think we're going to break his poor *Ami* heart by taking it off him, sir?' he queried.

'More like his head, you big rogue!' Steiner was businesslike again. 'Come on, Todt, let's waste no more time. It's just what we want.'

Swiftly the two of them began to cross to the back of the house, occupied by the American soldier with the gun.

'The longer this war goes on,' Patton declared to Hardt as they walked out of the CP to the waiting cavalcade, 'the more we're going to hear of that kind of crap. How Tech. Sergeant Joe

Zilch from East Overshoe, Maine, stuck his thumb in the dyke and stopped the bridge from collapsing, or how Colonel Wideass of Little Pessary, Ohio, led his men in a suicidal charge — to the rear. Human Interest, bah! Whoever heard of an American general replying to another commander with a word like "nuts"?'

Hardt grinned and made way for the General to get into the jeep. Patton was obviously angry that McAuliffe and the 101st were getting more publicity than his beloved Third Army, which had relieved the beleaguered garrison. 'Well, General, you know what they say — if you can't beat 'em, join 'em?'

'What do you mean?' Patton poised upright next to Mims, looking down at Hardt curiously.

'You'll just have to create an equivalent legend to Bastogne if you want to get the Third into the headlines back home.'

Patton's eyes narrowed thoughtfully for a moment. 'You might be just right at that son.' Then he turned to the driver. 'OK, Mims, take her away. Let's go and see if these sky boys have really been earning their pay these last couple of days!'

Slowly the cavalcade of high ranking officers and press correspondents started to draw away from the CP.

'Here they come, Major!' Todt whispered urgently. 'That convoy's lousy with scrambled egg.'

'But where are the big boys?' Steiner asked, squinting along the sight of the automatic rifle as the two of them crouched there on the edge of the flat roofed house overlooking Bastogne's main square, and watched the cavalcades come ever closer.

An armoured car passed, four frozen soldiers on its deck, their mittened fingers on the triggers of their grease guns. A radio half-track followed. Slowly a jeep began to turn into the battle-littered square. Todt caught a glimpse of a bright white Trench coat and a lacquered helmet, gleaming with three overlarge gold stars. 'That must be one of them!' he whispered. 'Three stars — *das muss doch ein hohes Tier sein!*'

A thin hard face came into the gleaming circle of glass of the telescopic sight. Steiner did not know who the American was, but as Todt had said he was a big wheel. He would die first. Slowly, almost lovingly, his right forefinger started to curl around the trigger.

'*Whoosh!*' With frightening suddenness, the Messerschmitt 109e came barrelling in at tree top height, its eight machineguns spitting fire at a rate of eight hundred rounds per minute.

'*Great Balls of fire!*' Limey cried in alarm. The bottle of stolen beer dropped from his nerveless fingers and shattered on the cobbles as the great black shadow trailed by the German fighter swept across the road. He flashed a bitter look of implacable hate upwards, 'You rotten sod, taking the drop of beer —' The words froze on his lips.

Two men armed with an automatic telescopic rifle were crouched on the parapet of the house opposite: two men in civilian clothes, whose faces seemed vaguely familiar. But it was not their faces which alarmed Limey at that moment. It was the rifle. It was pointed directly at Patton's suddenly stationary jeep! 'Dutchie — *the roof!*' he cried, unslinging his grease gun with frantic fingers as the Me 109e came zooming in once again at 400mph.

'The General — they're out to get Blood and Guts!' Dutchie moved quicker than he had ever done in his life before. He knelt down and unslung his machine pistol in one and the same movement.

'*Fire — for Christ's sake, fire at the sods!*'

But Dutchie never managed to press his trigger. With an ear-splitting, tremendous roar the fighter was on them, drowning their upturned faces in its evil black shadow. Machineguns chattered. Vicious scarlet flames crackled the length of its wings, as the tracer sped towards the two men crouched on the roof. Todt tried to make a run for it. He got a matter of feet before the slugs ripped his back apart. For a moment he staggered on, a shattered hand held out like that of a blind man's feeling his way, mouth wrenched open and gasping for air which would not penetrate a blood-filled throat! Then he pitched face downwards — dead.

Steiner made no attempt to run. He lay there calmly, accepting his fate, as if it had been ordained from the start. His body twitched violently as the slugs smacked into his back. Their impact flung him right over so that the last thing he saw on this earth was the crooked cross of the plane which had killed him. '*Stu ... pid,*' his colourless lips formed the one word. His head dropped to one side, mouth open absurdly, his sightless eyes full of the overwhelming knowledge that it had happened to him at last.

Patton surveyed the dead German machine gunner, with his outstretched hands holding a belt of ammunition in frozen supplication, for a moment more, before turning to face the shivering, blue-faced correspondents waiting for his final word of that long December day. 'Gentlemen,' he snapped, 'this afternoon you've seen Bastogne and heard a lot about its "battered bastards".' He spat out the words as if they were slightly obscene. 'Now I'm going to tell what the Third Army did this Christmas.'

Hardt grinned in spite of the freezing air. The Old Man was off again.

'During that time the Third Army moved farther and faster and engaged more divisions in less time than any other army in the history of the United States — possibly in the history of the world.'

McAuliffe breathed out hard, but Patton did not deign to hear him.

'Now that may sound like George S. Patton is a great genius. Actually he had damned little to do with it. All he did was to issue the order which was — "hit the sons of bitches in the flank and stop 'em cold".'

Abruptly Patton dropped his hand on Hardt's shoulder. 'And it was boys like this who did the hitting and stopped the Krauts.' Hardt blushed.

'With his men he battled his way here from Luxembourg, hitting the Hun time and time again, barrelling a path through to the "battered bastards of Bastogne" by main force. For six long bloody days my T-Force fought their way here to the sky boys along that highway — through hell.' 'Yeah,' he grinned, displaying his discoloured teeth, '*on a highway through hell*. And you can quote me on that one, gentlemen. Good-bye!'

As the guns began to roar and the infantry started to advance once more across the snowy fields in the slow careful manner of men, who knew their luck was running out fast, Hardt followed the General back to the jeep, a knowing grin on his exhausted face. '*Highway through hell*,' he muttered to himself and shook his head in admiration. The General had done it again — he had created a new legend.

Moments later the jeep had disappeared into the grey gloom of the new battle...

A NOTE TO THE READER

Dear Reader,

If you have enjoyed this novel enough to leave a review on **Amazon** and **Goodreads**, then we would be truly grateful.

Sapere Books

Sapere Books is an exciting new publisher of brilliant fiction and popular history.

To find out more about our latest releases and our monthly bargain books visit our website:
saperebooks.com